THE GETAWAY LOST IN TIME

A MYSTERY SEARCHERS BOOK

BARRY FORBES

THE GETAWAY LOST IN TIME

A MYSTERY SEARCHERS BOOK

VOLUME 7

By
BARRY FORBES

BAKKEN
BOOKS

ISBN 978-1-955657-24-2
For Worldwide Distribution
Printed in the U.S.A.

Published by Bakken Books
2022

PRAISE FOR BARRY FORBES

AMAZING BOOK! My daughter is in 6th grade and she is home-schooled, she really enjoyed reading this book. Highly recommend to middle schoolers. *Rubi Pizarro on Amazon*

I have three boys 11-15 and finding a book they all like is sometimes a challenge This series is great! My 15-year-old said, "I actually like it better than Hardy Boys because it tells me currents laws about technology that I didn't know." My reluctant 13-year-old picked it up without any prodding and that's not an easy feat. *Shantelshomeschool on Instagram*

Great "clean" page turner! My son was hooked after the first three chapters and kept asking me to read more... Fast forward three hours and we were done! *Homework and Horseplay on Amazon*

This is Nancy Drew collaborates with the Hardy Boys. There are enough twists and turns to remind you of driving on Fish Creek Hill. ... Take a break, wander away from the real world into the adventurous life of spunky kids out to save the world in the hidden hills of the Southwest. *Ron Boat on Amazon*

A superb and rip-roaring mystery read, and good clean fun! Forbes nails it, and I'm looking forward to the rest of the series. *Arizona customer on Amazon*

Virtues of kindness, leadership, compassion, responsibility, loyalty, courage, diligence, perseverance, loyalty and service are characterized throughout the book. I recommend all elementary and junior high school libraries should have a copy of this book. *Lynn G. on Amazon*

DISCLAIMER

Prescott, the former capital of the Arizona Territory, is considered by many to be the state's crown jewel. Aside from this central Arizona locale, *The Mystery Searchers* series is a work of fiction. Names, characters, businesses, places, events, incidents, and other locales are either the products of the author's imagination or used in a fictitious manner. Any resemblance to actual persons, living or dead, or actual events is purely coincidental.

Read more at www.MysterySearchers.com

For Linda,
whose steadfast love and encouragement
made this series possible

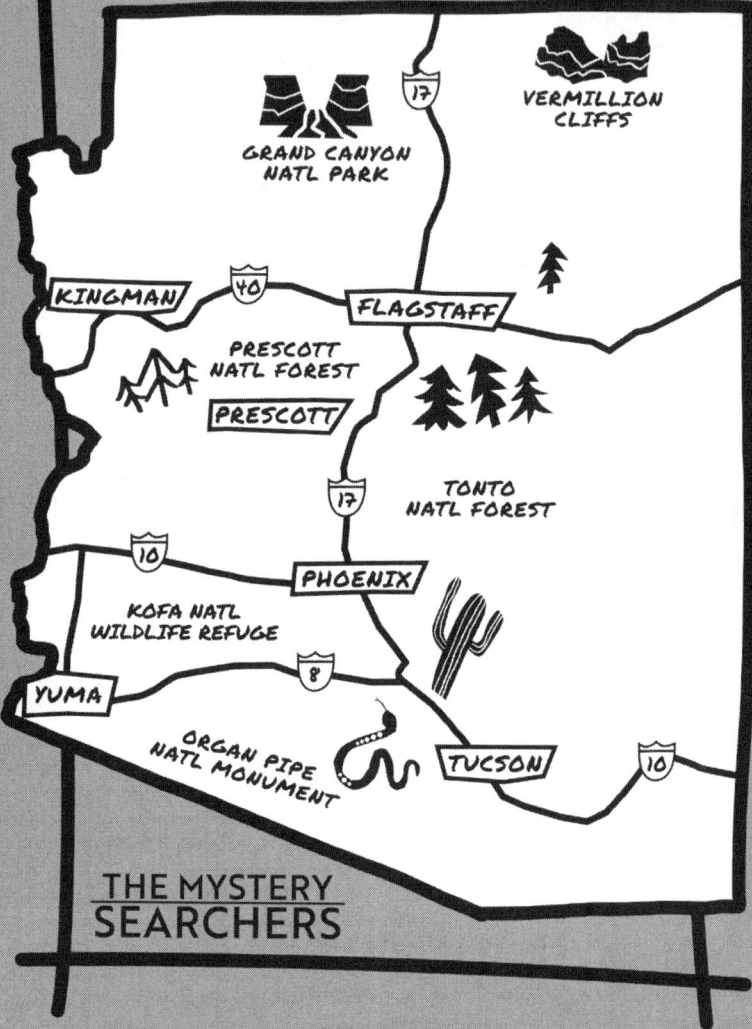

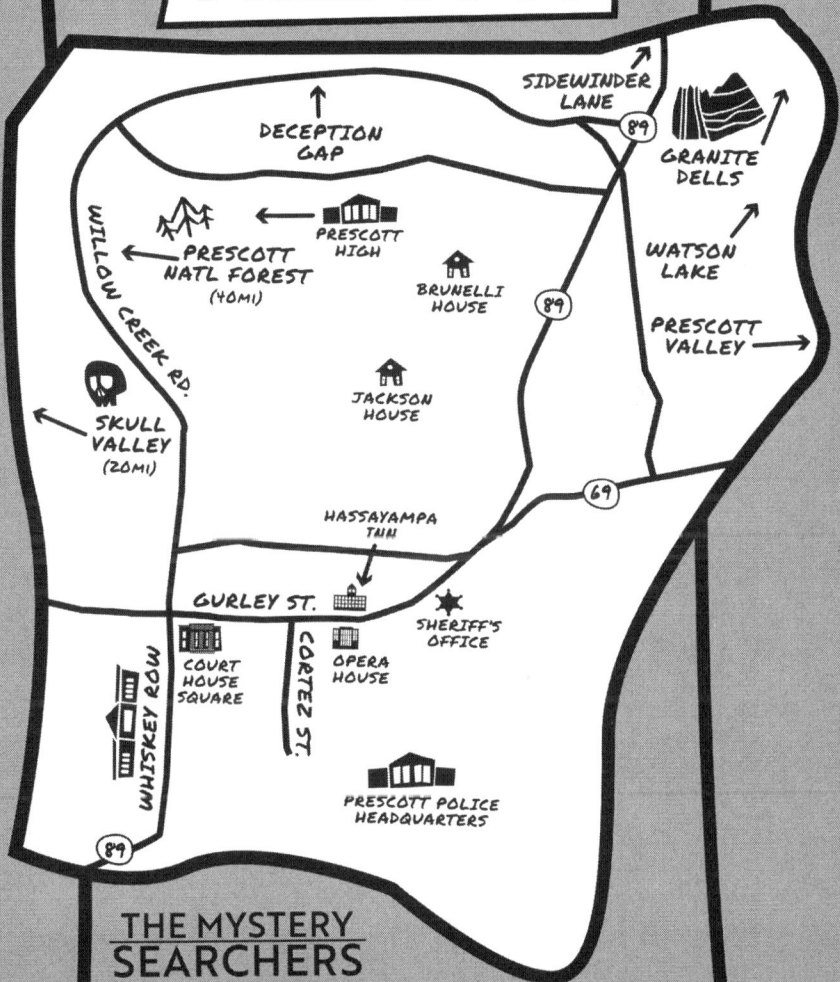

SURPRISE!

Suzanne nosed the twins' late-model Chevy Impala into a gravel parking lot at Watson Lake, a popular hiking destination in Prescott, north on Highway 89. It was Tuesday morning, two days after Christmas. Not long after eight o'clock.

The Jackson twins emerged into a bracing wind that whirled dead leaves around their feet. Dark, threatening clouds scudded past at a furious pace. Before them, acres of blue-grey water glinted as whitecaps raced across the lake's surface. Somewhere in the distance, birds screeched: a warning, perhaps, of a coming snowstorm, or freezing sleet. Or hail. Or worse.

"Suzie, you picked a wonderful morning for a hike," Tom grumbled. He thrust his hand up into the wind, feeling for moisture. Nothing—yet. He glanced up. "Those clouds could hammer us at a moment's notice."

"Lovely. Couldn't be better." Suzanne took a deep breath and threw her arms upward. True, it smelled like rain. And trees. And fresh air, all mingled together in a delightful outdoorsy fragrance.

The shoreline—punctuated by huge, rounded granite boulders, many of them half submerged—extended into narrow promontories flanked by tiny islands. In some places, pyramids of rock rose majestically, almost cliff-like, from the water's edge. Barren aspen trees, scattered around the lake, bent in the heady gusts.

"Can you *believe* it?" Suzanne declared. "Not another car in sight —we'll have the trail to ourselves." A sudden burst of wind pushed her long, brown ponytail aside. She zipped up the jacket of her dark-blue, fleece-lined jogging suit, a Christmas gift from her parents—warm as toast.

"Okay by me," Tom said. He pulled on a windbreaker, snug and water-resistant, just in case, then slung a canteen over one shoulder. "Let's go." Tom set off, angling left, pushing hard into the headwind, his sister close behind.

A five-mile hiking trail, guided by white dots along the pathway, circled a lake situated one mile above sea level. The better part of the path remained flat before climbing into a moderate hike that twisted and turned around the enormous boulders.

Nice, Suzanne thought, as a promontory provided momentary shelter from the biting wind.

Rounding a sharp turn in the trail, Tom turned and called out to his sister. "Careful, it's slippery here!"

A snowfall had blanketed the city early on Christmas morning, melting away by noon the following day. But with the chill in the air and a cold wind gusting strong and often, the snowmelt had refrozen into a thin glaze of ice in a few bare, rocky spots on the trail.

They trudged onward in silence, each bend revealing Watson Lake's hidden secrets. Fifteen minutes passed before something on a damp patch of ground caught Tom's eye, stopping him dead. He fell to one knee.

"What is it?" Suzanne asked.

"Mountain lion tracks."

"Oh, joy." She bent over beside him and peered straight down. "Yup. I hate it when you're right. Fresh ones, too."

Gazing at the rustic beauty that lay all around them, *isolated* and *lonely* were words that sprang to mind. But *danger?* No. Not at all.

Yet the twins knew from long experience in rugged central Arizona that hikers always had to be cautious about wildlife.

These prints left no doubt. A mountain lion's paw, front or rear, displays a distinctive triangular heel surrounded by four clawed toes. The top of the heel has two lobes, while the bottom has three. The elongated toes are like extended ovals. In the soft, wet earth, the tracks were a perfect match for the illustration the twins remembered vividly from their childhood scouting manuals. Not to mention previous hikes—central Arizona *is* mountain lion country, after all.

Tom stood. "As long as we stick together, the cat won't bother us."

They set off once more, both nursing a touch of apprehension.

A quarter mile later, they rounded a curve just in time to spot a tawny-colored flash of fur whip silently from one side of the trail to the other. Fifty feet ahead at most.

"What the heck—" Tom started. He came to a complete stop. "Did you see that tail?" he whispered.

"It's the mountain lion," Suzanne hissed. "Hiding between those boulders."

"*Seriously?*"

"Seriously."

The twins knew that attacks on humans were rare. And on two people hiking together? Never. *Still . . .*

Tom flapped his arms in the air. Mountain lions attack when their prey is small, but size and noise frighten them. "Beat it!" he yelled.

"Oh—my—gosh," Suzanne stuttered. "I can barely see it . . . Look, right behind the first boulder, on the other side of that bush. It's watching us!"

"'Never run from a mountain lion,'" Tom murmured. That adage —drilled into them since childhood—had popped into his mind.

"Back away . . . easy," Suzanne urged. "If there's any movement, scream."

"Boys don't scream."

"Try."

The twins edged backward, ever so slowly.

Then, seemingly out of nowhere, a medium-size dog rushed from behind the twins, brushing between them as it beelined toward the predator. The dirty white mongrel with grey splotches stopped a few yards before the boulders where the cat was hiding—the top of its head, ears straight back, was only just visible—barking and growling, loud and menacing. It paced in a semicircle, eyes locked onto the visible patch of tawny fur.

Seconds later, the dog quit barking. The mountain lion had backed off and loped silently away.

Gone.

"Dang!" Tom exclaimed.

A NEW FRIEND

E arlier that same morning, Suzanne had experienced a sudden realization, and an unpleasant one, at that.

My favorite season of the year, she reflected, *has come—and gone.* The pungent smell of pine needles didn't help, either—it was nothing more than a sad reminder. *Another Christmas past,* she brooded. The twins' mother, Sherri, an at-home social services worker, was on a phone call in her office. Meanwhile, their father—Chief Edward Jackson of the Prescott City Police, known simply as "the Chief" to everyone but his own family—had rushed away in the middle of the night. Something about an emergency on the city's west side.

Suzanne traipsed into the kitchen and found her brother at the breakfast table, engrossed in *The Daily Pilot,* Prescott's local newspaper. "Dad was called away in the middle of the night? What's that about?"

Tom's eyes never left the paper. "No clue."

Suzanne sighed. It didn't help that the twins' best friends, Kathy and Pete Brunelli, had spent Christmas with their cousins in Anaheim, California—yet *again.* Same story every year, an annual ritual. They wouldn't return until the next day, Wednesday the twenty-eighth. In the evening. Late.

No mystery to pursue, either. The vanishing at Deception Gap had wrapped up at the end of summer, just days before the new school year began. Suzanne's mind returned to the railyard at Deception Gap and the bizarre ordeal of Beau Bradley. *Wow, that was a great case. Wish we had one now.*

She poured a cup of steaming hot coffee for herself, adding a splash of cream before glancing over to her brother. "Want more?"

"Mm-mm." He shook his head, lost in the sports page.

"It's awfully quiet when the Brunellis aren't around, isn't it?"

"Uh-huh."

"Earth to Tom . . ."

He looked up. "What?"

"Let's do something."

Tom shrugged. It was still early, right after breakfast, and the family had stayed up late watching their favorite Christmas movie, *It's a Wonderful Life.* "Like what?"

"Like hiking around Watson Lake," Suzanne replied brightly.

Tom yawned without replying.

"Am I boring you?"

He turned the page. "Not at all. I'm doing just fine, thank you."

"Well, have fun."

His sister was persuasive, to say the least. Barely fifteen minutes later, the twins were heading north on Highway 89 with Suzanne at the wheel. It was a winding, fifteen-minute drive through Arizona's scenic red-rock country. Traffic was light—as in close to zero.

Tom bent over in the front seat, lacing up his hiking boots. "You know what, Suzie? You can be pushy without even trying."

"Darn good thing," she said, cracking a smile. "Who wants to sit around all morning and do nothing?"

"That was my plan, actually."

The Jackson twins—tall and willowy, with light brown hair and brown eyes—had been born and raised in the central Arizona city of

Prescott. The city reminded some people of the Old West, surrounded as it was by high desert and rolling hills, with mountainous country not far away, close to the immense Prescott National Forest—and renowned for historic Whiskey Row and the world's oldest rodeo. Still, many locals figured it was a sleepy little place where not much happened.

True. Unless your father was the chief of police. That changed things. A lot.

Even as a small child, Suzanne radiated a natural energy that threatened to burst free at a moment's notice. Her innate curiosity about life was legendary, and when friends thought of her, words like *confident* and *outgoing* came to mind. But there was another word too.

"As long as your *temper* doesn't get in the way," her mother had warned. Often too. But over the years, Suzanne's childhood nickname—"Spitfire"—had faded. Still, there were times . . .

Suzanne's twin brother, by contrast, had a quiet, thoughtful nature. Tom fought hard to overcome a natural shyness—a trait easy to ignore when they were together, as they often were, because his sister was the exact opposite. As he grew older, technology had made all the difference. For Tom, tech was, well, intuitive. He had learned to code in grade school and became a founding member of Prescott High's prestigious technology club in his freshman year—the same year their team won a national robotics competition.

"He's the only one in our family who understands remotes," his sister had quipped at the time. "That's huge."

Now, not half an hour after they had parked and begun their hike, a fearless mongrel had dashed in to save the twins from a potentially dangerous encounter with a fearsome predator. The dog turned and approached them, warily. He drew closer, still cautious.

Suzanne had stopped breathing without even realizing it. She exhaled sharply.

"He doesn't want much to do with us," Tom said. He knelt on the hard path beside his sister.

"I get it. He's frightened. Someone was mean to him."

"Could be. But he sure knows how to handle mountain lions."

The dog continued to inch his way forward until he was close enough to sniff Suzanne's hand.

"Aren't you something?" she asked, gently touching the top of his head.

"He likes girls," Tom said, reaching over to pet him too. "Your timing was perfect, boy. You look like a cross between a husky and a German Shepard. What's your name, boy?"

Soon enough, the dog had accepted the twins. He wagged his tail and licked Tom's nose. They were friends.

"He doesn't have a collar, so . . ." Suzanne ventured.

"How old do you think he is?"

"Four or five," she guessed.

"Where's his owner, I wonder?"

They stood and gazed both ways along the trail. There wasn't another soul in sight.

Suzanne said, "I'm sure he's lost."

"Let's see if he follows us."

AN HOUR AND A HALF LATER, THE TWINS HAD COMPLETED THE circular hike with the wind at their backs and the dog leading the whole way. They crossed into the gravel parking lot to find five other cars parked nearby, but still no people.

"They must be on the trail . . . or kayaking," Suzanne said.

A tiny kayak floated far out in the middle of the lake. Thunder rumbled somewhere in the distance. The wind kicked up once more, and a strong smell of rain permeated the air.

Tom glanced upward at the dark, threatening clouds. "Once the deluge starts, they'll be beating a path back here."

An unmarked Jeep Grand Cherokee pulled in and parked behind them. A uniformed officer stepped out of the SUV. "Good morning, how are you?"

"Doing great," Tom answered. The dog growled. Suzanne knelt and put an arm around him.

"I've been trying to catch this stray for a couple of days," the officer said. "No way could I get close to him—he took off every time. I think it's the uniform."

"Any idea who owns him?" Suzanne asked.

"Nope. Someone must have deserted him out here. Folks reported seeing a grey-and-white dog and even left food on the trail. But he wouldn't let anybody near him, would you, boy?"

The mongrel barked.

"I'm surprised he's taken to you. How did you find him?"

The twins laughed. "We didn't," Tom replied. "He found us." They described their encounter with the mountain lion.

"Imagine that," the officer said, chuckling. "Well, thank goodness this guy came along. Are you taking him home?"

"Yes!" they chorused.

"Good for you," he said, smiling. Before leaving, the officer asked for a name and phone number. "In case the owner shows up." When he heard their names, he realized who they were. "Hey, you're the Jackson twins. I work for your dad. Fine man, the Chief." He soon drove off.

Suzanne opened the Chevy's back door, and the dog jumped in. The twins ducked into the front seat, with Tom at the wheel this time.

"He didn't like the officer one bit," Suzanne said. "Maybe he was right—it's the uniform."

"Who knows? He sure likes us." Tom glanced over at his sister. A frown had crossed her face. "What's the matter?"

"Dad won't like this. He'll want to run the dog over to the county shelter."

"Yeah, likely," Tom agreed.

Their father wasn't an animal lover. The dog, panting in the backseat, stuck his head between the front seats and whined.

Suzanne shook off the thought. "That's okay. Mom will side with us." She petted the dog's head and received a sloppy kiss in return. "What should we call you, buddy?"

"You know, he could be microchipped," Tom warned his sister.

There was a long pause. "I never thought of that."

"If he is," Tom said, "the chip will probably tell us his name. And his owner, maybe even an address."

The skies opened. A deluge hammered them all the way home.

3

REX

On Wednesday morning, the Jackson family gathered around the breakfast table. The twins' father poured himself a second cup of coffee. "Last time I counted, we've had two dogs, three cats, and a bird. That's enough."

To their amusement, the dog—lying between Tom and Suzanne on the kitchen floor—growled.

He had already barked at the Chief that morning. *Twice.* "He doesn't like uniforms," Tom mouthed to his sister.

"But Dad," Suzanne argued, "you couldn't ask for a braver dog..."

Two minutes later, Sherri ended the ensuing argument with a pronouncement: "Edward, this beautiful dog saved our children from a mountain lion. No way is he going to the pound." She knelt to pet the pooch and kissed him on top of his head.

Her husband groaned, stood up from the table, and marched off to work.

At just the same moment, Mrs. Otto—the Jackson family's friend and neighbor—rapped on the back door. The sound of a barking dog caused her to rush over and check out the new addition to the family. She had a ton of experience with pets; among her many interests, she was famous for running her own personal menagerie. Dogs, cats, birds, fish, turtles—"

"You name it, Mrs. Otto had sheltered them," Suzanne recalled with a giggle. "Remember the snake?"

"He's a beauty," Mrs. Otto said, stroking the dog and receiving a wet kiss.

"He took to you in a heartbeat," Suzanne said approvingly.

"You need to have a vet look him over, just to be on the safe side," Mrs. Otto advised the twins. "He'll also check to see if there's a microchip. I've used Dr. Ritter for years. He's the best veterinarian in town."

The twins' mother, Sherri, tapped his name into her laptop and logged into his online calendar for booking appointments. "He's got an opening today at three o'clock."

RIGHT ON TIME, THE TWINS MARCHED INTO A SMALL, STERILE examination room that reeked of antiseptic.

"Good morning, nice to meet you," Dr. Richard Ritter said. He had an open, easy manner, a sparse frame, and thin, greying hair, and he appeared to be in his early sixties. The twins shook hands with him as his eyes trailed over the dog. "Well, who do we have here?"

The stray barked and tried to back away. *It's the dark blue scrubs the vet's wearing*, Suzanne realized. *Another uniform.*

"No clue," Tom replied. He knelt and pet the dog to settle him down. "We found this guy wandering around Watson Lake all by himself."

"Yesterday morning," Suzanne explained. "He got between us and a mountain lion on the trail. Scared the cat off."

"No kidding?" Dr. Ritter said, sounding impressed. "Good for you, boy. Put him on the scale—let's check his weight."

The digital display registered sixty-eight pounds.

"Lift him up on the examination table, would you please."

The dog growled again as the twins boosted him onto the stainless-steel tabletop. The vet ran his experienced hands across the dog's head and ears, then down his flanks and along his abdomen. His eyebrows arched up. *"Wait a minute. . .* I've seen you before, haven't I? Let's see if you've got a microchip."

Suzanne's eyes widened in surprise. "You recognize him?"

"Well, he looks familiar," the vet replied. "But I'll treat up to a dozen dogs every day, so..."

Dr. Ritter opened a cabinet door and retrieved a handheld scanner. He scanned side-to-side, starting just behind the dog's head. "If he's a got a chip, it should be in the fatty tissue behind one of his shoulder blades. No bigger than a grain of rice." The scanner beeped. "There it is."

Five minutes later, after an online query to the national pet microchip database, Dr. Ritter turned back to the twins. A strange look had crossed his face. *"I can't believe it,"* he said.

The twins glanced at each other. "You can't believe what?" Tom asked calmly.

"You found Hilda Wyndham's dog!"

"Who's Hilda Wyndham?" Suzanne asked.

"Didn't your read the newspaper this morning?"

"Well, uh..." Tom started.

"Just a sec," the vet said. He raced out of the office, returning just seconds later. He threw the morning edition of *The Daily Pilot* on the metal table. "No wonder he looked familiar. Say hello to Rex."

A small image of the dog had made the front page, right beside a woman identified as Hilda Wyndham.

"That's him!" Suzanne exclaimed. "Rex? That's his name?" The dog barked.

"It sure is," the vet replied. "In fact, I'm the one who microchipped him four years ago."

The headline in *The Daily Pilot* caught the twins' attention. "Woman's death is labeled 'suspicious' by medical examiner." Next to it was a picture of an elderly woman with shocking white hair and a half-smile. A second heading, accompanied by a smaller picture of a dog, read, "Have you seen Rex?"

"Oh, my goodness," Suzanne said, her finger lodged on the photograph. "That's him—that's Rex—for sure! So the county sheriff has been looking for this guy?"

"That's what the story says," the vet replied. "They don't say 'why' Hilda's death is suspicious, but somehow the dog disappeared at the same time. . . the day before Christmas, first thing in the morning."

"Sheesh," Tom said. "Just two days ago. Where did the owner live?"

"Outside the city limits, north on Highway 89. . . in the country, a few miles the other side of Watson Lake. A neighbor found her lying on the kitchen floor."

"Judging from her picture," Suzanne said, "you'd think that would be a natural death. How old was she?"

"Well," Dr. Ritter replied, squeezing his nose in thought, "I haven't seen her for some time. But I'd guess she was in her eighties."

Tom shook his head. "Somehow, I missed that story in the *Pilot*."

"That's because your nose was buried in the Sports section," Suzanne bugged.

Tom shot her a look before checking for the name of the reporter. "Hey, look. Heidi wrote the story," he said to his sister.

"Last time I saw Hilda for Rex's annual checkup, she was a healthy, active lady," Dr. Ritter said. "We got along real well. Anyway, I only deal with sick animals, not sick people. Too bad Rex couldn't talk—he knows what happened out there, don't you, boy?"

The dog whined, then barked once more.

Suzanne's mind skipped ahead. "I'll bet the surviving family members are missing him."

"I doubt it," the vet replied. He shone a light into Rex's ears, then ran his hands over the dog's belly again. "The story says there's no known next of kin." He paused as he checked the dog's teeth and took his temperature. He returned the scanner to the cupboard and dropped the thermometer into a liquid-filled glass. Then he pulled off the rubber gloves and tossed them into a chrome garbage can with a flip-top lid.

"There's nothing the matter with Rex," the vet concluded. "Looks healthy to me." He petted the dog, only to receive another growl. "Do you plan on keeping him?"

Suzanne's heart skipped a beat. "Yes, we sure do."

"Well, you've got yourself one smart animal. Brave, too. It's not every dog who'll take on a mountain lion. There're a lot of cats up north on Highway 89—that's rugged country. I'll bet he's come face to face with a few of them."

He smiled and shook hands with the twins. "Bring him back in a year."

Rex jumped off the examination table and barked once. Time to go.

4

SOMETHING STRANGE

"Who knew?" Suzanne hissed, glancing sideways at her brother as they walked out of Dr. Ritter's office.

"Yup," Tom replied. "Another full-blown mystery—from out of nowhere." He opened the rear door of the Chevy, and Rex jumped in. The twins slipped into the front seat.

"Crazy," Suzanne declared. "Wait until the Brunellis hear about this. We find a lost dog and he leads us to a mysterious death. I mean, what are the odds?"

Tom, always cool and collected, showed a rare level of excitement. "Pete and Kathy are back tonight. Text Kathy and fill her in. Right now, we need Heidi."

YEARS EARLIER, HEIDI HOOVER HAD IMMIGRATED TO THE U.S. FROM Mozambique with her family, refugees from the country's civil war. She had attended Prescott High, graduating a few years ahead of the twins and their two best friends. A compact young woman with tight black curls, Heidi wore a habitually bright expression that expressed her dynamic personality. After college, she had landed a job with Prescott's hometown newspaper, *The Daily Pilot*, where she soon emerged as the paper's star reporter—and one of the mystery searchers' biggest fans. The foursome had shared numerous mysteries with Heidi, with each adventure landing them on the *Pilot*'s front page.

"You guys don't give up easily," she liked to say. "I like that."

Suzanne placed the call, which went straight into the reporter's voicemail. "Hi, this is Heidi Hoover at *The Daily Pilot*. Got a tip? Please leave a message." *Beeeep.*

"Heidi, it's Suzanne. You wrote a story about Hilda Wyndham who died under suspicious circumstances. We want to know more. Call me."

"I'll give her sixty seconds," Tom said, chuckling. The twins knew the reporter well.

He wasn't far off. Two minutes later, Heidi's voice was crackling over Suzanne's cell phone speaker. "How on earth did you get involved in Hilda Wyndham's case?"

The twins filled Heidi in, ending with Suzanne switching the call to Facetime and holding the phone toward the dog to introduce him. "Say hello, Rex."

To everyone's surprise, Rex barked happily. They all laughed.

"Well," Heidi said, "believe it or not, after Hilda Wyndham's death, two neighbors searched high and low for Rex. The woman lived out on 89 north—number four Sidewinder Lane. It's a small community, only ten properties total. Smack in the middle of nowhere, bordering federal land."

"Sidewinder Lane," Suzanne repeated, grimacing at the very thought of the road's namesake. Snakes were definitely not her favorite creatures. "Who'd ever want to live there?"

Heidi chuckled. "No one could figure out what happened to the poor dog," she continued. "So he's been wandering around Watson Lake for two days?"

"It looks that way," Tom replied. "A park ranger told us that hikers had reported a stray dog. You'd wonder how he got there—and why."

"Not only that," Suzanne added, "but Rex is skittish; he doesn't like people in uniforms."

"Including Dad's," Tom said with a grin.

"But he frightened off the mountain lion," Suzanne added, "and made friends with us. Go figure."

"Why don't you come down to the newspaper offices? We'll get a shot of Rex and you guys for a short follow-up story. And I'll fill you in on the mysterious death of Hilda Wyndham."

NOT MUCH LATER, REX WAS POSING WITH THE TWINS FOR A PICTURE in front of *The Daily Pilot* building. He took an instant liking to Heidi.

"What a beautiful dog," she crooned, running her hands through his soft fur. "Mmm, nice shampoo aroma. Did you guys just give him a bath?"

"Uh-huh," Suzanne replied. "And he liked it too." The twins had bathed Rex earlier that morning, turning his dirty smudged coat into bright white with handsome splotches of grey.

"Follow me," Heidi said.

The twins, with Rex following behind, trailed the reporter down a corridor and into the newspaper's glass-enclosed conference room. Rex curled up at Suzanne's feet and fell sleep.

"Here's the scoop," Heidi said, plunging in. Anyone could tell that she loved her job. "Hilda Wyndham's death was downright weird. 'Suspicious death,' the Sheriff's Office called it. Picture this: Christmas Eve morning, about 10 a.m., a neighbor finds her dead, lying on the kitchen floor, and calls nine-one-one. After the medical examiner appraised the body at the scene, he labeled it a *sudden* death, pending an autopsy. That could mean almost anything: sudden onset of illness, choking, an accident, an overdose. Like when an elderly person dies without warning."

"That makes sense," Suzanne deduced. "She was in her eighties, right?"

"Eighty-five, but the neighbors said she didn't look a day older than seventy. Walked three miles with Rex twice every day, all four seasons. The one neighbor who's a friend told me that she ate organic food, took vitamins, and exercised on her bike. Next thing you know, she's dead without a mark on her."

"She died instantly?" Suzanne asked.

"The medical examiner ordered an autopsy, which concluded no," Heidi replied, shaking her head. "It showed that Mrs. Wyndham suffered a cardiac arrest, fell unconscious, and died a few minutes later."

"If she died of a heart attack," Tom asked, "why is the law involved?"

"Well, it's a . . . *conundrum*," Heidi said with a smile, using a word she knew was one of Tom's favorites.

"How did the case get changed to a 'suspicious death'?" Suzanne asked.

Heidi's button nose twitched. "It was Sheriff McClennan. You know what he's like—he smelled a rat. He wondered who took Hilda's dog—and why. The neighbor who found Hilda claimed that the dog would *never* leave her, dead or alive. The sheriff found that suspicious and ordered the crime scene crew to sweep the house. Just in case."

She paused. "There were two coffee mugs in the sink, still a little damp. A sharp-eyed crime-scene tech took them back to the lab and ran a few tests. Guess what?" She leaned closer to the twins, her voice dropping lower in a conspiratorial hush. "They found a tiny trace of a rare, powerful drug, carfentanil, in one of the mugs."

Tom was already searching the internet on his phone. "Carfentanil . . . used to tranquilize elephants. . . a chemical weapon, and a street drug—"

"*Awfully* bad stuff," said Heidi.

"The mugs were just *sitting* there?" Suzanne asked.

"Yup. One imprinted with the word *Hers* on a cactus-flowered background, the other marked *His* over a high-desert trail scene. Guess which one had residue of the drug in it?"

"Hers," Suzanne said flatly.

"Bingo."

"*His* and *Hers*," Tom said. "So the sheriff figures the suspect is a male?"

"It's a guess."

"Would the *His* be Mrs. Wyndham's husband's mug?"

"Who knows? His name was Troy, and he died forty-five years ago."

"Well, I've never heard of carfentanil," Suzanne said. "It certainly points to a suspicious death."

"Uh-huh." She stopped. Heidi had a provocative habit of leaving people hanging.

"Well," Tom prompted, "that's when they found the poisonous drug in her body, right?"

Heidi ignored the question, another trait that drove people nuts. "You remember Dr. Brent Walker, the medical examiner for Yavapai County, right?"

"Oh, sure," Suzanne said. A tall guy with a serious demeanor, she could picture him easily. "We met him a couple of cases ago, when we were working on the treasure in Skull Valley case. Remember, Tom?"

"Sure. I'll never forget him. He surprised the heck out of us."

"Better get used to it," Heidi teased, giggling at the memory. "That's him. A by-the-book guy. Knows his stuff."

Tom nodded. "Okay, got it. It looked like she died of natural causes, but the autopsy found the drug in her system, right?"

"Wrong. He said there was no doubt: Hilda died after suffering a heart attack, the exact opposite of what the sheriff expected."

The twins glanced at each other. "None of that stuff in her body —*at all?*" Tom asked.

"Zero. *Nada.* Not even a trace."

Something wasn't adding up. "Wait a sec, Heidi," Suzanne blurted. "What about the residue in her coffee mug?"

"The sheriff suspects that someone intended to bump Mrs. Wyndham off—that the drug residue is proof of intent. But she collapsed and died from a cardiac arrest before the deed occurred, *not* from sipping the doctored coffee. The coffee never touched her lips."

Suzanne was almost speechless. "That's crazy!"

"Yup. Sheriff McClennan thinks he might be able to get the guy on a felony charge, basically terrifying someone to death—if they can find him. Weird, huh? A nice old lady like that."

"Who would do such a thing?" Suzanne said. "The poor woman collapses in front of some creepy guy trying to do her in—from fright!"

"Let me get this straight," Tom said. "Someone's in Hilda Wyndham's kitchen—the day before Christmas, early in the morning—about to have coffee with her. But he's really there to poison her with a powerful drug; in fact, he's already poured the stuff into her mug—"

Suzanne interrupted. "We can't be sure it was a man just because she served him coffee in a mug with *His* on it."

"Sure," Tom continued. "Anyway, she falls to the floor—from a heart attack—and dies in minutes. And the murderer is so careless that he fails to cover up the intended crime. . ."

"Suspiciously so, I'd say," Suzanne said.

"Uh-huh. You got it," said Heidi. "That's the sheriff's theory, and he's sticking to it."

Suzanne raced ahead. "Even if they could catch the guy—if it is a guy—how could the county prove it?"

Heidi shrugged. "No clue."

"What about Rex?" Tom asked. "How does he fit into the story?"

Heidi focused on the sleeping dog. "There's no doubt he must have been in the kitchen, likely right at her feet, when she dropped to the floor. The sheriff's theory is that the perp dragged off the only witness to whatever happened to Hilda Wyndham, then dumped him somewhere near Watson Lake."

The twins looked down at their dozing furry friend as Heidi's words sank in. In the background the tap-tapping of multiple keyboards filtered through the open door.

In Suzanne's mind, an image formed of some nasty individual dragging the shattered dog away from his mistress and his home. *Perp* was too a nice a word for the perpetrator of such an evil deed. No wonder some people spooked Rex. *Not all people,* she thought. *Just the ones wearing uniforms.*

Tom spoke next. "Why would someone drag off an innocent dog?"

"That's what the sheriff wants to know," Heidi replied. "The neighbors searched everywhere. And then, days later, you guys show up with him." Her eyes grew larger, she moved closer to them, dropping her voice even lower.

"This is weird, but. . . it's like. . . *you're the ones meant to solve this mystery.*"

AN INVITATION

Pete and Kathy bounced into the Jacksons' kitchen, right after breakfast on Thursday morning. The Brunellis—with their coal-dark hair, olive-hued skin, Italian-American to the core—had arrived home the previous evening. Shorter and a little heavier than their tall, willowy twin friends, the Brunelli siblings looked enough alike to be mistaken for twins too. The foursome had been inseparable since their early days at elementary school.

"Where is he?" Pete demanded. Rex, sleeping on the living room sofa—the Chief had left earlier—heard the commotion and pranced into the kitchen, just as friendly as could be.

Kathy fell to her knees to pet the dog. Rex whined and licked her hands. "Boy, you sure smell good, and you're gorgeous too."

"Hey, great to see you guys," Tom said, high-fiving his best friend. "Timing is everything—we've got a new case."

"Copy that," Pete said, leaning over to pet Rex. The dog licked his nose. "We read Suzanne's message: new dog, new mystery—and they're connected. Intriguing. What's to eat?"

Kathy asked, "So, someone tried to poison the poor woman?"

"Yes," Suzanne replied.

Together the twins raced to fill in the Brunellis on everything they had learned about the mystery so far.

"Who's got the case?" Kathy asked.

"Sheriff Steve McClennan," Tom advised.

"Yeah!" Pete said, raising one arm in celebration before he buried his head in the refrigerator.

The foursome had known the sheriff of Yavapai County as a colleague of the Chief's since childhood. More recently, they had worked with him on two other cases.

Pete dropped a piece of bread into the toaster and helped himself to coffee. He poured a cup for his sister. *Just like home.* And it was. The four had grown up in each other's houses.

Sherri walked in and hugged the Brunellis, then retreated to her office.

"So, what's next?" Kathy asked.

"The sheriff wants to meet Rex," Suzanne said.

"And us," Tom added, "with Heidi. He called half an hour ago, after he heard we had rescued Rex."

"Sounds more like Rex rescued *you*," Pete replied.

"That's the truth," Suzanne said.

Kathy asked, "When's the meeting?"

"As soon as we can get out there," Tom replied, glancing at the kitchen clock.

Pete popped the toast.

BARELY HALF AN HOUR LATER, THE FOUR MYSTERY SEARCHERS AND Heidi strolled through the front doors of the Yavapai County Sheriff's Office. To the obvious amusement of the staff, Rex trailed behind as the group tripped down a long corridor and straight into a spacious office.

Sheriff McClennan, a large, beefy man dressed in a khaki uniform, stood and walked around his desk, extending his hand to everyone. "Hello, hello! Great to see you all again. So this is the missing Rex?" He ignored his ringing phone and leaned over to pet the dog's head. Rex backed away and growled at him.

"Oh, c'mon fellow," the sheriff said. He fell to one knee and held his hand out. "I'm a dog lover, you can trust me." Rex edged toward him warily before licking the sheriff's hand.

Suzanne shook her head. "It's the uniform, Sheriff. For some reason he has a problem with people who wear one."

"I'll bet anything he can just tell who likes dogs," said Heidi, "and who doesn't."

"Well," the sheriff said. "I've got two mutts at home and I love them to death." He scrunched down and scratched Rex's belly as the dog rolled over. "So you're a survivor, huh?"

The twins explained about Rex's aggression to the officer they had met at Watson Lake, and to the Chief.

Sheriff McClennan guffawed. The Chief had been his friend for decades. "Your dad told me he chased away a mountain lion at Watson Lake. How great is that? There aren't a lot of dogs who'd take on a big cat—they're dangerous. Sit down, make yourselves comfortable."

The sheriff circled back to his desk. Everyone found a seat and Rex sprawled across the floor, resting between the twins with his head on his front paws.

"You've been searching for Rex?" Pete asked, opening the discussion.

"Sure have. Maybe he can lead us to whoever is responsible for Hilda Wyndham's mysterious death. When one of Mrs. Wyndham's neighbors didn't see her walking Rex that morning as usual—"

"—he stopped over to check on her," Kathy said, "and found her lying dead on the kitchen floor."

Heidi said, "I clued them in yesterday, Sheriff. I told them about the lab report and autopsy too."

"Great," said the sheriff. "Then you also know that the victim's neighbors say that Rex would never leave Hilda's side, alive, or dead. So—"

"Someone dragged Rex away, and dumped him at Watson Lake," said Pete.

"Downright strange," the sheriff said with a nod. "Plus, there wasn't a single fingerprint on the kitchen table or countertop, the coffee mugs, not even the handle on the kitchen door. The guy wiped down everything."

"But careless in one critical detail?" asked Tom.

"Uh-huh," Sheriff McClennan said. "The drug."

"We looked it up already," said Suzanne. "Carfentanil is a synthetic opioid. They use it in Africa to tranquilize elephants. It's a hundred times as potent as fentanyl, which makes it ten thousand times stronger than morphine."

"Deadly," continued Pete, "especially when purchased on the street from drug dealers, which is happening right now in too many states."

"You've done your homework," said the Sheriff, sounding impressed. "But this the first time we've seen it here in this part of Arizona."

"Like all opioids," continued Kathy, "the drug slows down all the functions of the central nervous system, especially breathing. A miniscule amount is all it takes. You're dead. Fast."

"And you don't have to drink it," Tom added. "It can be absorbed through the skin or inhaled in powder form."

"And someone slipped it into her drink," Heidi concluded.

"*Stirred* it in too," the sheriff said. "Our lab identified residue on a spoon in the sink."

The sheriff waved a hand toward the now sleeping dog. "Rex is our only eyewitness, but he's not talking."

"But, Sheriff, what about motive?" Suzanne asked. "Who would want to bump off a nice elderly lady living out in the middle of nowhere? What threat could she pose to—to *anyone?*"

"Ah, good questions. That's why I asked you all to stop by." The sheriff shifted his bulky weight on the office chair, causing it to creak. He leaned forward, scanning their faces. "I'm short on manpower. You've earned a reputation for solving mysteries, and this is a strange one. Her neighbors say Hilda Wyndham couldn't have had an enemy in the world. Although one neighboring couple looked out for her, no one really knew her well. The woman was almost a recluse. But Rex worshipped the ground she walked on."

At the sound of his name, the dog's head popped up.

"Wait a sec," Kathy interjected. "She's having coffee with an individual in her kitchen, early in the morning. That means she must have known *that* person well."

"That our belief," the sheriff replied confidently.

"Which is weird," mused Tom, "for a recluse. She trusted that individual enough to offer him a seat at her kitchen table. That's no stranger, for sure."

"Correct." Sheriff McClennan leaned forward again. "Someone frightened the poor lady to death. Hilda Wyndham deserves justice, and I intend to see she gets it."

Unnoticed, Rex had risen and sat up on his haunches. He barked, twice.

"Motion accepted," Kathy quipped. Laughter rippled around the room, releasing the built-up tension.

"We're all for helping, Sheriff," Tom said. Where do we start?"

"I'll have County Detective Derek Robinson meet you on Hilda's property," the sheriff replied, "this afternoon at three o'clock. He'll take you on a guided tour. Make sure you take Rex with you. No telling what he'll turn up."

Heidi asked, "What can I do, Sheriff?"

"Newspaper coverage," he replied grimly. "Lots of it. Put the story on page one as much as possible. I'm hoping that your reporting hasn't spooked the murderer. . . that he hasn't fled town or left the state."

"Mrs. Wyndham died five days ago," Suzanne said. "Maybe the trail's already cold."

The sheriff stood and walked over to a window, gazing out. The morning clouds had darkened, and an outside Arizona state flag snapped in a brisk wind. A few sparse raindrops splattered the glass with a leaden sound. He turned toward them, his face set in stone.

"Maybe. . . maybe not. Either way, whoever did this awful thing needs to feel the heat. I'm betting he figures he got away with it. He's comfortable, he thinks the worst is behind him. So—"

"—So let's turn it around and make him *real* nervous," Heidi said.

"Flush him out of hiding," said Tom.

"Force him to make a mistake," added Kathy.

"Right," said Sheriff McClennan. "Get the message out: Yavapai County isn't about to give up on this case. . ."

"Hilda Wyndham is crying for justice!" finished Pete with a flourish.

"I like that," Heidi said, scribbling like mad. "'Hilda Wyndham cries for justice.' That'll be tomorrow's headline."

"Perfect. Nervous criminals make negligent errors." The sheriff drew a circle in the air with his index finger. "That's how we'll reel him in."

An image popped into Suzanne's mind: a heartbroken dog, lying next to Hilda, guarding the body of his beloved mistress. *No way would he have left her.* Fighting a rush of emotion, she reached down to pet Rex. He licked her hand.

The sheriff stood and walked round his desk to the dog. He leaned over. "What secrets could you tell us? What did you see? Who did it? We need your help, buddy."

6

NUMBER FOUR SIDEWINDER LANE

Tom navigated Highway 89 as the morning's foul weather drifted into the afternoon. The temperature had dropped and sleet, whipped by howling winds, swirled around the Chevy.

Stormy winter days in Prescott weren't that common. Even when it snowed, the white powder would often melt away over the next day or two. Sleet was worse.

"There's no traffic out here," Suzanne observed, peering out through the rhythmically sweeping wiper blades with strained eyes. Visibility had dropped close to zero. She checked the map app open on her mobile.

"No kidding," Pete said. "No one wants to drive in this stuff."

"Including Rex," Kathy said with a giggle. The dog whined as he sat between the Brunellis in the backseat.

"So Heidi couldn't make it?" Pete asked.

"Nope," Suzanne said. "She's on another story but wants us to call her later. We're almost there, Tom. Sidewinder Lane is the next turnoff to your left—right . . . *there.*"

Tom cranked the Chevy hard onto a frozen gravel road and jolted along through a community of high-desert properties dotting both sides of the road. Hilda Wyndham's ten-acre property, they were told, would be fourth on the left. A minute later, they turned onto a private dirt road with a posted sign: No Trespassing.

"Nice," said Kathy.

"The sign?" her brother asked.

"No, silly. The house. It's so quaint."

A single-story clapboard house, creamy white with dark-blue trim—probably many decades old to judge from its style, but well kept up—emerged from the driving sleet. To its left and right were towering elm trees. A double garage, set back a few feet to the right, partially concealed three other structures: a barn and two smaller buildings, all in a row, side-by-side. A four-door sedan sat empty in front of the house.

"That's gotta be Detective Robinson," Pete said.

Tom pulled up behind the unmarked car, and everyone got out into the icy rain, zipping up their jackets. Rex beat Kathy out of the car, jumping over her and racing to the front door. A man of medium height and curly red hair, wearing a trench coat over a two-piece suit, came out to greet them and usher them inside. He had a humorous air about his eyes and a jutting, square jaw. The dog zipped past him and through the open door.

"Hi," the detective called out, his freckled hand outstretched. "I'm Derek Robinson. You must be the mystery searchers. I assume that was Rex?"

Introductions followed.

"Since we'll be working together, please call me Derek," the detective said, flashing a smile.

"We're glad to meet you," Suzanne said.

"Likewise. Come on in. Where did that dog go?"

The small house turned out to be a single-story, mid-twentieth-century rambler. The group strolled into the living room, which was neat as a pin, with one sofa and two easy chairs—a hanging lamp between them—all arranged around a coffee table. A tall, narrow bookcase, stuffed tidily full, rested beside one chair. Religious images decorated three walls, and an eight-by-ten framed photo stood on a small side table between the chairs.

"Is that Hilda in the photo?" Kathy asked, indicating a petite brunette who was shown hugging a smiling man, with a young boy nestled between them.

"It is," the detective replied. "That's Troy Windham, her husband, beside her, and the little guy is Robert, their son. That shot is easily sixty years old."

A copy of *The Daily Pilot* lay on one sofa, folded up, still in its plastic sheath. "The morning newspaper from the day she died," Derek said, pointing to the unopened daily. "We're having her mail forwarded to the Sheriff's Office." He led them into the kitchen to find Rex lying in front of the refrigerator. "Well, look at that. He's right where her neighbor found Hilda's body."

Rex whined and placed his head down on his front paws.

"The neighbor found Hilda in front of the refrigerator?" Kathy asked.

"That's correct. The medical examiner said she had died two hours earlier."

"Who's the neighbor?" Tom asked.

"Dave Ratzinger. He and his wife, Sarah, live on the next lot to the west, same side of the lane. Hilda walked Rex past his front window every morning and evening. He told us she never failed to wave. When Hilda didn't show up that morning, he came looking."

"What about the other neighbors?" Pete asked.

"Dave and Sarah Ratzinger are the only adult contacts she seems to have had for years. They kept an eye on her—just because of her age, and her living alone."

"*No* one else?" asked Suzanne softly.

"A young neighborhood kid named Jack Watson stopped by occasionally to say hi to Rex here, but Dave guesses she hadn't received another visitor in many years—since her husband passed. Troy died young, in his early forties. Robert, the boy in that photo, also died young, eighteen years ago."

All Kathy could say was, "Wow."

A long moment passed in silence.

"The morning she died," Tom asked, "Mr. Ratzinger never spotted a car in her driveway?"

"No visibility from his house," Derek answered, indicating the westward view through a window lashed with rain and hail. "Burt Moore, the guy across the lane, noticed a dark, late-model car in the driveway, right around six a.m. A few minutes later, he realized that Rex was barking, but he paid no attention. Turns out he hates dogs —and children. Later, he peeked over again: the car had left. No one else spotted anything unusual. We checked."

"No security cameras?" Tom asked.

"Unfortunately, no," the detective replied. "With a few exceptions, these are mostly seniors, and country people aren't too much into security cameras. Besides, who needs them out here? There hasn't been a reported crime in the past decade. I checked. Plus, this road is a dead end—the only people who use it live here."

"How many?" Kathy asked.

"Ten couples. No children except the Watsons—they've got a boy named Jack."

"Tell us about the clues you've found so far," Pete said. "We know about the drug residue."

"That's the only one," the detective lamented. He gestured toward the kitchen countertop, where detergent and a sponge holder stood neatly beneath a small cup hook. "The two mugs were sitting upside down in the sink when our deputies arrived. The perpetrator rinsed them out with soap and dried them a bit with a clean dish towel we found hanging on the stove's handle. But he didn't scrub them hard enough."

"We heard about the *His* and *Hers* decoration on the mugs, and the spoon," Suzanne said.

"So there's no doubt that Hilda's visitor came into the house," Pete said, eager for new information.

"None," Derek said. "But we don't have a clue who her visitor was—"

"Because you've found zero fingerprints," Tom concluded.

"Right," said Derek.

32

"Nothing else?" Tom asked.

"Nothing definite," the detective replied. "Burt Moore—the guy across the lane—had a feud with Mrs. Wyndham in the distant past. He told me they hadn't said a word to each other in twenty years."

"Interesting," Suzanne said. "That would be about twenty-five years after her husband died. . . and before Robert passed away. Did he say what the feud was about?" Suzanne asked.

"She accused him of spying on her," Detective Robinson replied. "According to Mr. Moore, she didn't like anyone even *looking* at her place. Which is hard not to do, as he mentioned—he basically lives across the street. If what he said is true, her reclusiveness had gotten extreme many years ago."

"Did you doubt him?" Kathy asked.

"Well, every person is a suspect—"

"Until you rule them out," said Pete.

Derek replied with a half-smile. "The guy's a little rough around the edges. I never met his wife—she refused to see me. I'm running a background check on them."

"Anything else?" Pete asked.

"Nope. At least nothing out of the ordinary. We took this place apart and put it back together. Frankly, we're at a loss. The sheriff pulled some of the manpower away—too many other cases to pursue. But he wants this one solved, so I'm still on it. And now, so are you."

They toured the rest of the house.

"Less than a thousand square feet," Tom declared. "Tiny rooms."

"You could eat off the floors," Kathy remarked.

A single hallway led to a bathroom and two bedrooms. The first bedroom featured a soft pink bedspread over a single bed and matching walls, a dresser, a bedside table with a small stack of books and a single lamp. Clean and neat. Opening the closet doors revealed clothes all carefully organized.

"Hilda's bedroom," Suzanne remarked quietly, tilting her head sideways to read the titles of the books.

Rex had slipped into the second bedroom without anyone noticing. He sat in a corner, staring as they entered before barking twice.

"What the heck," Pete said. "Is he trying to tell us something?"

Hilda had turned the second bedroom into a library, its four walls lined with bookcases, each one methodically crammed full. Suzanne, a book lover, was impressed. Once a week, she priced used books, a part-time job she cherished, at Prescott's St. Vincent de Paul Donation Center. Her manager there was Mrs. Otto, the same next-door neighbor of the Jacksons who loved animals.

Suzanne's eyes sped across the titles. "Hilda loved history, and some of these are old classics. I can't wait to go through them."

"Please do," the detective said.

Someone knocked on the front door. Rex barked and beat Derek down the hall.

"Hi, Dave," the mystery searchers heard the detective saying as they piled into the hall behind him. "Come on in. I've got some people you'll want to meet."

As the visitor walked through the doorway, Rex leapt up and almost bowled him over, pressing his front paws against the bib of the man's rancher-style overalls.

"Take it easy, Rex," the big man said, laughing. "I missed you too." He squatted down and allowed the dog to lick his face, tearing up before wiping his eyes with a handkerchief.

Everyone headed into the living room. Their guest shook hands with each of the four mystery searchers as Derek introduced them, explaining that Tom and Suzanne were the ones who had rescued the dog.

"Call me Dave. Thank you for bringing Rex home. I can't tell you how grateful I am. Where did you find him?"

"We were hiking at Watson Lake," Tom replied, "and ran into a mountain lion on the trail. Rex chased the cat away."

"Ah, yes. Rex has lots of experience with big cats, don't you, boy? He hates them. Every year he's chased one or two from the neighborhood. He's famous for it. Mind if I sit down?"

Derek said, "Please do." Dave settled into one of the easy chairs.

Rex trotted over and laid his head across the man's knee. He massaged the dog's ears. "I promised Hilda years ago, if anything ever happened to her, I'd look after Rex. He loves it out here, don't you, boy? And he loves me too. We go all the way back to the day he arrived."

The mystery searchers exchanged glances.

We're cooked, Tom figured.

Suzanne blanched. *Bye-bye, Rex.*

7

THE MYSTERY DEEPENS

The detective grabbed the other easy chair. Pete sat on the floor, while the others crowded onto the sofa.

"Dave knows what we believe happened in here," Derek explained as a way of introduction. "And Dave, these are the mystery searchers. They've got a track record in this area, and I need help."

"Well, I hope you're successful," the rancher responded, tugging at the bib of his overalls. "Whoever visited Hilda must have scared the poor woman to death. Sure, she had a few years on her, but . . ."

Tom asked, "Sir, what can you tell us about Mrs. Wyndham?"

"Not much, I'm afraid," he replied. "She was a very private person. Seldom talked about herself, or her past. Heck, I couldn't even guess where she came from. I just assumed she was an Arizona native."

"Born and raised in California," Derek interjected. "Moved here after her marriage."

"Tell us what you know about her family," Kathy prompted.

"Doesn't have any. Her husband died long before my wife and I retired here. Never met the guy. Her son, Robert—"

"Do you know what Robert died from?" Pete asked.

"Heart issues, she told us at the time." Dave sat bolt upright. "Say, that's something, isn't it?"

"You mean, maybe heart trouble ran in Hilda's family?" Kathy asked.

"Yeah." He paused for a few seconds. "Anyway, Robert was a single guy—never married. Quiet like his mom, always pleasant to me. He died two years after my wife and I moved in. Lived here with his mother until he passed."

"That library of Hilda's must have been his old bedroom," Kathy said.

"Sure was," Dave replied.

Suzanne was dying to ask a question. "Rex barks at people wearing uniforms. Has he always done that?"

A quizzical look crossed the rancher's face. "Never."

"Never?"

"Not that I recall. . . nope."

Pete wondered, "How did they support themselves? Did they work?"

"Hilda didn't. Robert ran a bookstore downtown, on Whiskey Row."

"That explains the library," Suzanne remarked.

"So Mrs. Wyndham never worked?" Tom asked.

"Not since I've known her. That never came up in our conversations."

"You talked to her often?"

"Well, sort of. We'd spot her walking Rex twice a day. In fact, it got so that we looked out for her passing by. That way, we knew she must be okay." The dog whined again before Dave reached down and nuzzled his pointy nose. "Over the years, if she got stuck, I'd do the odd construction job for her. Put in new kitchen cupboards just last month. Getting her to talk wasn't easy, but Hilda and I always got along well."

Kathy said, "We understand she never had company."

"Not once in twenty years that I'm aware of. Of course, her house isn't visible from where I live, so who knows? And there were deliveries. . . but in the last few years she ordered everything online, including her groceries, and had them dropped off on her doorstep."

"She didn't go into town?" Suzanne asked.

"Once in a long while. Doctor, dental and vet appointments—things like that."

"And the morning she died," Tom asked, "you didn't see a strange car on the road?"

"Nope."

The detective, listening and taking notes, interrupted. "The guy across the street noticed a dark, late-model car in the driveway, right around six a.m. Next time he looked, it had disappeared."

"That would be Burt Moore," Dave said. "He and his wife, Barb, have an unobstructed view into Hilda's property. The Moores never got along with her. They haven't talked in years. She told me they spied on her."

"Did they?" Pete asked.

"I doubt it. Hilda could be . . . difficult if she didn't like you. My wife and I were the only friends she had."

The discussion ranged on for another hour, but nothing shed light on the mystery. Soon, Derek wrapped up the meeting.

"C'mon, Rex, let's go home," Dave said.

Suzanne held back tears as she gave Rex a big hug goodbye. Her brother and the Brunellis took turns petting the dog once more. Without saying a word, they all realized there was no choice.

"Bye, buddy," Tom said. It saddened him to lose the dog, but Rex appeared overjoyed. He raced off, running circles around Dave.

"Let's check out the rest of the property," the detective said after Dave and Rex were out of sight.

They headed out into a freezing grey afternoon. Over the past hour, the wind-driven sleet had died to a whisper of its former self. First up was the two-car garage, half of which was empty space, the other half occupied by an old-model Ford sedan.

Pete peered through the driver's side window. "Clean as a whistle, not many miles on the odometer. She didn't drive much."

"Right," said Derek. "We ran the plates. Of course it's hers. Nothing unusual in there."

They toured the barn—spacious and bare with a dirt floor, it appeared to have been unused for years. The other two buildings revealed little. One was an empty storage shed, the size of a small garage, the other a similar-size workspace with a wall-to-wall bench, a pegboard packed with dusty tools above it, and neatly stored garden and lawn equipment, including a riding mower.

The group stepped back outside and circled the three outbuildings. Behind the barn sat a faded-yellow Caterpillar digger, old and rusted out, mired six inches in the ground.

"This thing hasn't moved in decades," Pete said. "And check out the tractor."

A small, tarnished green John Deere tractor rested beside the digger, stripped of parts: a derelict.

"The house is so tidy inside," remarked Suzanne, "but these vehicles are wrecks."

"I wonder why they needed them?" Kathy said.

"This was a farm at one point," Derek replied. "If you look out here, due south, there's nothing but flat, empty land. Behind it is a service road that extends east and west past all of these properties along Sidewinder Lane. And on the other side of the road is federal government land that goes on for miles."

His cell phone buzzed. A minute later he announced, "Gotta run. Here's my card, and here are the house keys. You have free access to the property. See if you can find anything unusual. Right now, I'm at a loss. There's only one avenue I'm pursuing."

"What's that, sir?" Tom asked. The four friends all felt great respect for police officers.

Derek squinted before answering. "Well, I'm wondering about Hilda Wyndham. . . like, who is she really?"

"Me too!" Pete exclaimed.

"Think about it," the detective continued. "She's hidden out here for years—"

"No friends, no relatives," added Tom.

"A posted No Trespassing sign," Kathy continued, "and she seldom went to town."

"She wouldn't even tell Dave, the only adult she ever really talked to, where she came from," Suzanne said.

"And she worried about her neighbors spying on her," Derek finished. "What does that say?"

"She was hiding something!" the mystery searchers chorused in unison.

"Exactly," Derek replied, nodding. "We ran her fingerprints, but nothing came back. No warrants, she never served time. But I can't help wondering: Who is she? What's her background? Why the low profile? Is it possible someone from the distant past caught up with her?"

"Someone," Suzanne said in an ominous tone, "who wanted her dead?"

THAT EVENING, THE FOURSOME GATHERED AT THE JACKSONS' HOUSE and sprawled out in the living room. The Chief strolled in and found a spot on the sofa. The mystery searchers filled him in on the day's events.

When they got to the part about Rex, the Chief grinned. "Gee, that's too bad."

"Not nice, Dad," Suzanne objected, pulling a face. "We love that dog."

"We sure do," Sherri agreed as she walked in and sat down beside her husband. "But you weren't friendly to the poor thing, were you?"

"Hey, the dog's happy, right? Who's complaining?" the Chief replied, raising a hand in self-defense.

Suzanne couldn't wrap her mind around something. "You know what, Dad? Dave Ratzinger, her friend out there, told us that Rex *never* barked at people in uniform."

"That is so weird," Kathy said.

"Well," the Chief said, "he sure enjoyed barking at me."

"And every other uniformed officer," Pete noted.

"Have you met Detective Derek Robinson?" Tom asked his father.

"I haven't. But he enjoys an excellent reputation, and the sheriff speaks highly of him."

"What about our theory?" Kathy asked. "That Hilda Wyndham had a past that caught up with her—"

"And did her in!" Pete said.

"Sounds like you're onto something. What have you got to work with?"

"Not much," Pete admitted. He explained about the mugs, and the drug residue—"something called carfentanil."

The Chief's head snapped up. "*Carfentanil.* That's a new one around here. Very dangerous."

"Something else," Suzanne added. "The woman's a recluse, except for being friendly with Dave Ratzinger and a young kid named Jack, but she's having coffee with some guy early in the morning on Christmas Eve—in her kitchen. It tells us she knew him. *Well*, in fact."

The Chief grunted in agreement.

"He also wiped all his prints clean in the kitchen," Kathy declared. "That's suspicious. It points to a calculating criminal."

"One without a conscience," Suzanne added.

"I agree," the Chief replied.

"How do you know the suspect is male?" Sherri asked.

Tom replied, "She served coffee in *His* and *Hers* mugs."

"That's hardly definitive," the Chief said.

"True," Pete said.

"There's a room packed full of books," Suzanne said. "We'll go through them tomorrow looking for clues."

"Did you walk the property?"

"Not all of it yet," Tom replied. "The place is enormous—ten acres. That's next on the schedule too."

"I'd also talk to *all* the neighbors," the Chief advised. "Who knows? You might pick up on something the Sheriff's Office missed."

"I'm a little nervous about this case," Sherri protested. "Someone tried to poison the poor woman."

"Oh, Mom," Suzanne said. "You worry too much. There's safety in numbers. We'll be careful."

"Uh-huh, sure. I've heard that before," her mother countered. "But whoever this person is, he's dangerous."

The Chief, aware that his twins planned to go into law enforcement, always encouraged their interest in mystery solving. "Just keep in touch with Detective Robinson. You'll be fine."

8

CLUES

The Friday morning edition of *The Daily Pilot* slammed onto the Jacksons' driveway and skidded to a stop. Tom had risen early, waiting patiently as he nursed a hot cup of coffee. He raced out into the chilly morning and flipped the newspaper over.

There it was, and on the front page too. He zipped back into the house. "Hey, Suzie!" he shouted as he spread the paper across the kitchen table.

Suzanne took the stairs two at a time and darted into the kitchen. "Hey, yourself." She glanced at the headline. "Oh, wow. Heidi came through."

It read, "Hilda Wyndham cries for justice." The twins read the story together in silence. Heidi covered the known facts of the case and ended with a plea for help from the public:

Someone attempted to poison Hilda Wyndham, and Sheriff Steve McClennan of the Yavapai County Sheriff's Office is determined to find the perpetrator. "I want your readers to know," the sheriff said, "that we believe the intimidation of this woman led to her cardiac arrest. At the very least, the male suspect deserted a person knowing she was ill or dying. We also found evidence of a dangerous drug. My office won't rest until we bring this individual to justice."

The male suspect left behind clues that the Sheriff's Office is pursuing. In addition, Prescott's own mystery searchers, a foursome that has solved multiple mysteries in the past, have joined the case. If anyone has information regarding Hilda Wyndham's untimely death, please call the tip line at the Yavapai County Sheriff's Office.

THE CHIEF CAME INTO THE KITCHEN AND READ OVER TOM'S shoulder. "That's interesting. Now the perp knows you're involved."

"Can't hurt, right?" Suzanne asked.

"Depends," their father replied. "He might know who you are; if he doesn't, he can search online and figure it out." He lowered his voice, knowing that Sherri would see red flags if she heard him. "Be vigilant—I'm sure he won't like you poking around."

"We will," said Suzanne.

"The good news," the Chief continued, "is that he'll realize the sheriff is serious about nailing him. Even better, the article says there are other clues: what clues did the perpetrator leave behind?"

"He doesn't know," said Tom.

"That's right. And *that* could stir him into risky actions he wouldn't normally take. One mistake on his part and . . ." The Chief didn't have to finish.

The Brunellis called. "Boy, oh boy," Kathy said. "Heidi came through big-time, didn't she?"

"For sure," Suzanne agreed. "What's our next move?"

AN HOUR LATER, THE FOURSOME PILED INTO THE CHEVY AND HEADED out on Highway 89 with Tom at the wheel. A sea of low, overhead clouds threatened over the distant mountains; a westerly wind blew with no sign of snow or sleet. They arrived at the Wyndhams' home just after 9:00 a.m.

Suzanne and Kathy plunged into the house, prepared to wade through the hundreds of books in the spare bedroom. "We should be able to comb through them in one day," Suzanne said.

"Let's do it," Kathy said. The place was freezing. "Someone shut off the heat." She flipped the thermostat to On and pushed up the temperature a few degrees.

"While you're combing," Pete said, "we'll walk the land."

"Have fun."

The boys bundled up against the freezing wind and split up, marching across the largely open fields south of the buildings in a systematic parallel zigzag. The land undulated up and down a bit but was overall quite level. It was obvious, as Derek had told them the day before, that at some time in the past, the acreage had served as farmland. That would explain the lack of any significant rocks anywhere on the land.

In the center of the property was a stand of barren cottonwoods, their leaves long since blown away. Tom disappeared between the enormous trees before yelling out, "Hey, check this out!"

Pete hustled over. "What is it?"

A well-used pathway led between the cottonwoods into a park-like area centered around a tiny pond, partly ringed with a built-up earthen berm. Overlooking it was a well-worn two-person wooden bench. Wind whistled through the giant branches. A damp smell of decaying greenery filled the air.

"Nice," Pete said. "It's like an oasis in here."

"You bet, Hilda's oasis," Tom said, "and she's been here recently too." He pointed to footprints in front of the bench made by someone with tiny feet.

Pete picked up a small rectangular card lying face up in the dirt. "She dropped a prayer card . . . Someone died."

Tom peered over his shoulder. "Her son, Robert. Sad. That's really old then." A faded picture displayed a cross illuminated by the sun, accompanied by a common prayer for the dead. Pete tucked the card into his pocket.

The two continued to walk the property, but nothing else captured their attention. They soon made their way back into the warm house.

"Anything?" Kathy called out.

"Nothing but a scenic oasis," Pete replied.

The boys came into the library and described finding the pond. . . and a prayer card.

"Here," Pete said, handing it to his sister. "For her son, Robert."

"That tells you a lot about Hilda," Kathy said, turning the card over in her hands. "I'll bet she was a special person."

"If this dates from Robert's death," Suzanne said, taking the worn card from Kathy's hand, "then it's eighteen years old. It must have been very precious to Hilda. Why on earth would she drop it out there and leave it?"

"Bet anything it fell out of a prayer book," Kathy said.

"How's it going?" Tom asked, noting an enormous pile of books on the floor.

"Nothing yet," Suzanne replied. "Why don't you guys search the other rooms?"

"Okay," Tom said. "We'll start in the kitchen."

The boys took the kitchen apart, checking every cupboard. Dishes, pots, pans, silverware, and place mats were all flipped over and returned to their original positions. A couple of the cupboard drawers contained paper, pencils, pens, erasers, safety pins, and tape. A small pad of lined yellow paper caught Tom's attention.

The four-by-six-inch pad lay upside down at the very bottom of the last drawer, under a pile of seemingly random bits of paper—recipes, receipts, notes. Tom paged through the pad's handwritten notes. On the last page, he found what looked like some kind of handwritten appointment: day, date, and time, with two initials.

"Bingo!" Tom shouted as he tossed the pad down on the kitchen table. The girls heard him and rushed into the kitchen.

"Whatcha got?" Pete asked.

"Evidence."

"Tell us."

Pete and the girls circled around the yellow pad.

Tom read aloud, "'D.R.—Saturday, December twenty-fourth, six a.m.'"

"That's the morning Hilda died!" Suzanne exclaimed.

Kathy asked, "Who's 'D.R.?'"

"The guy who tried to poison her, of course," her brother replied dryly.

"Dave Ratzinger," Suzanne said, "that's who." She paged through the pad, flipping through grocery lists, to-do lists, indecipherable notes, even a Bible quotation. "Hey, here's another one . . . from Monday, November sixth, eight a.m.: 'D.R.—replacing cupboards.'"

Tom remembered. "So that's when Dave replaced her kitchen cupboards, as he told us—"

"So 'D.R.' *has* to be Dave," Kathy interrupted.

Silence blanketed the room. Suzanne winced. She couldn't help but like the guy.

"Hold on," Kathy protested. "Rex doesn't have a problem with him. Under the circumstances, I'd say that's a big deal."

More silence.

"That's the truth," Tom said. "Rex loves him."

"I'm confused," Suzanne said, throwing a hand up. "And I'm getting a headache."

The boys continued in the kitchen, while the girls returned to work in the library, fanning out each book, looking for anything written in the margins, hoping something interesting might fall out from between the pages.

It wouldn't be the first time that treasure had surfaced from a book. Suzanne's part-time job at the St. Vincent de Paul Donation Center had led to a forgotten tintype of a Confederate war officer. The thrift store sold it for seventy-five dollars. Once she had found an eighty-year-old birth certificate. And, just last winter, a pristine hundred-dollar bill had popped out of a famous historical novel, dating back to the 1920s. Best of all, however, was the previous summer, when a map had fluttered to the floor out of an old classic, a *treasure* map that led to one of the mystery searchers' most intriguing cases: the treasure of Skull Valley.

The girls set aside old books in one pile—Suzanne planned on checking them later for their value, thinking maybe they could be donated to St. Vincent de Paul. And they replaced newer books on the shelves in the same position where they found them.

Not much later Kathy cried out, "Look what I found!"

In her hands she displayed a large book-box—the kind with a spine and front cover that appeared to be an antique book, but with a cover that opens to reveal a hidden storage area. Inside were about two hundred old photographs and three sheets of yellowed paper stapled together and folded in three.

Suzanne unfolded the document. *"Her will!* Nice!" Suzanne exclaimed softly. "Now we've got something."

Kathy spilled the photos out gently onto the carpeted floor and spread them out with the fingertips of both hands. "There's even a bunch of old black-and-white pics."

Suzanne's attention was drawn away from her reading. "Uh-huh, just like the house. Mid-twentieth-century."

"Is this Hilda?" Kathy held the picture up a young child, appearing to be ten or eleven years old.

"Oh, for sure. You can see the resemblance in the living room picture. Look at all that black hair."

"Here she is with her husband and a young boy."

"Gotta be Robert, five or six years old."

The two of them rooted through the photographs, flipping through time as years and decades flew by. Hilda's husband started off as a slim, blond-haired young man with a thin face. As the years slipped away, he began putting on weight at the same time as his hair thinned.

Their boy, Robert, grew into a winsome young guy who had inherited his father's features and blond hair.

"Hey, look at this," Kathy said. "He and his buddy parked in front of Prescott High."

Suzanne craned her neck. "You're kidding, right?"

"Nope. He beat us to the school by fifty years, give or take."

"Yikes. He would've been older than our parents."

The boys appeared in the bedroom doorway. "That's pretty darn old," Pete said.

"Don't let Mom hear you say that."

"What did you find?" Tom asked.

"A treasure trove of photographs," Kathy replied.

"Plus an important document," Suzanne said. She picked it up again and read the title aloud. "'The Last Will and Testament of Hilda Marie Wyndham.'"

"Oh, boy," Pete said. "Now we'll learn who her relatives were—are—whatever."

"Listen to this," Kathy said. She held up a three-by-five-inch recipe card from the bottom of the pile. Someone had handwritten a Bible quotation, noting the book and verse in the Old Testament source, and penciled in a tiny heart above it. "It's from Ezekiel 18:31."

"Ezekiel? Wait!" cried Tom. He dashed into the kitchen, returning seconds later with the little yellow pad, flipping madly through the pages. "I didn't think it mattered when I saw it before, but look: the same quote." He held out the pad for the others to see.

"Read it out loud," Pete urged.

Suzanne and Tom read aloud in unison, almost like a prayer: "'Cast away all the crimes you have committed, and make for yourselves a new heart and a new spirit! Why should you die . . . ?'"

9

A SECRET

Seconds ticked by before Pete broke the strange interlude. "We were right..."

"Meaning what?" his sister asked.

"Meaning," Pete continued, "Hilda Wyndham had something to hide."

"And the past caught up with her!" Tom said.

Suzanne chimed in. "A nice woman in her eighties? That's hard to imagine, isn't it? What could she have done?"

"You got that right," Kathy replied. "'The crimes you have committed'? What the heck?"

"Whatever it was, it troubled her," Suzanne said. "Enough that she found comfort in this Bible verse. See the heart she drew?"

"Hang on," said Tom. "We're not certain yet that this is her handwriting. Or that the verse refers to *her* crimes. Maybe she felt guilty over something someone else had done—her husband maybe?"

"She lived alone for the last eighteen years," Pete said. "Gotta be her writing. And—she did end up dead."

Kathy rolled her eyes. "I don't think the verse refers to *physical* death."

Tom quickly scanned Hilda's will—a simple document only three pages long. "Oh, my gosh."

"What?" his sister asked.

"She left everything to Dave Ratzinger and his wife Sarah! House, land, money in the bank account . . . and Rex."

Pete clasped his hands together. "Clinch! There you go. That explains the attempted murder—"

"We don't know that," Kathy admonished him.

"You don't *know* anything," he shot back.

"Something . . . doesn't add up," Tom said.

Just then a dog barked, and someone knocked on the front door.

"Rex!" Suzanne shouted, jumping to her feet. The foursome raced to the front door. Sure enough, Rex sat outside, peering in. A boy with a cowlick of blond hair flopped over his forehead stood behind the dog.

"Hi!" he called out. "My name's Jack. I live down the lane."

"Oh sure, Jack Watson," Tom said. "Detective Robinson told us about you." He pulled the door open. "Come on in."

Rex raced in and received a flurry of hugs. He managed to lick everyone's face before padding into the kitchen and flopping down on the linoleum floor. The four friends introduced themselves to Jack and shook hands with him.

"I know all about you," he said in response. "You're the mystery searchers. I've read about you in *The Daily Pilot*."

Pete couldn't help himself. He puffed up but tried not to show it. "Well, Jack, we need all the help we can get."

"Especially this guy," Kathy quipped, poking her brother.

Jack flashed a boyish grin, his piercing blue eyes widening as he searched each of their faces.

The mystery searchers liked him.

"How old are you, Jack?" Suzanne asked.

"Eleven going on twelve. And I love mysteries too. I've got the entire Hardy Boys series at home."

"My favorite," Tom said, giving the boy a high-five. "I've read every one of them."

"I liked Nancy Drew," Suzanne declared.

"The Famous Five," Kathy added, "a British series. Check it out. We read them all."

"Did you know Hilda?" Pete asked.

"Mrs. Wyndham? Oh, you bet I did. We were good friends. I came over and played with Rex a few times a week. This morning Dave Ratzinger asked me to take the dog for a walk. Rex got ahead of me and raced right to her front door. He was awfully close to Mrs. Wyndham, you know."

"Detective Robinson mentioned that," Suzanne said.

Jack glanced over to the twins. "Hey, I read that you were the ones who found Rex at Watson Lake. He worried us—me and my dad searched everywhere. So did Dave."

"*He* found *us*," Tom explained, "and chased away a mountain lion."

"That figures," Jack said. "Rex doesn't like cats one bit."

Kathy said, "So everyone tells us! Did Mrs. Wyndham have any other friends?"

"Not that I ever saw," Jack replied. "Just me and Dave, I guess. My parents called her a recluse, but she was awful nice to me."

Suzanne studied his blond hair and boyish features, and thought about Hilda's son, Robert. "What about the other folks out here?"

"Same," he replied. "Except for Mr. Moore across the lane. She didn't like the guy. Me neither. He's a grouch—always yells at me when I walk by his place. I ignore him. He hates dogs too."

"No one else?"

"Nope."

"Ever notice anything unusual out here?" Suzanne quizzed.

"Here? Nah—nothing ever happens on Sidewinder Lane." He shook his head. "It's quiet as a mouse. Boring too."

"Jack, could you do us a favor?" Tom asked.

"Oh, you bet," the boy replied. "How can I help?"

"Keep a watch on this place. If you spot anything out of the ordinary, or if something comes to mind, please let us know." Tom wrote his cell phone number on the yellow pad, ripped off a sheet, and handed it to the boy. "Call or text anytime, day or night."

"Will do," Jack replied.

They could tell he liked that.

Jack thrust the note into a pocket in his jean jacket. "Well, gotta go. C'mon Rex!" The dog bounded out of the kitchen and led the way out front.

"Boy, what a nice kid," Kathy said after the door had closed behind him.

"For sure," Suzanne replied. "No wonder Hilda liked him. He looks an awful lot like her son, Robert—blond hair and all. Let's try to finish the books."

The boys went back to work too. There wasn't anything else of interest in the kitchen. They attacked the living room, removing pillows and turning chairs upside down, hoping to find more clues that the crime scene techs had missed.

"I'm sure the sheriff's guys already did this," Pete said.

In Hilda's bedroom, they looked over the stack of five books on her bedside table, all with bookmarks: one work of fiction—the famous classic *Wuthering Heights*—and three historical nonfiction tomes centered on Europe in the eighteenth century.

"Man, she read five books at a time, swapping back and forth between them," Tom said.

"Yup. Kathy does the same thing," Pete said. "Weird, huh?"

"What did you say?" Kathy called out.

"Nothing!"

Meanwhile, the girls continued to plow through the photos. They divided them into decades and even individual years as best they could, starting with the black-and-white images and progressing through the decades. Hilda and her husband filtered through their teenage years as singles, then as a handsome couple who aged gracefully over time.

Most of Robert's photos were in color. From a baby to a toddler, he grew into his teenage years, then older. In his late teens, he picked up a buddy, another young man—same height, similar build, with thick black hair. They played ball, shared meals, worked on the land around the house, and swam in a pond.

"I'll bet that's the oasis," Suzanne pointed out. "The trees were a lot smaller back then."

Then the friend disappeared.

LATER, JUST AS THE FOURSOME PREPARED TO LEAVE, A CAR PULLED into the driveway.

"Detective Robinson—Derek," Pete said.

Derek parked behind the Chevy and strode over to the front door.

"How are you all doing?" he called out before stepping into the house.

Over the next half hour, they filled in the detective.

"Nothing yet in the photos," Suzanne reported. "But her will was in the book-box."

"You found her will? Good for you. I couldn't even locate her attorney."

Tom handed the document over to the detective. "She didn't use an attorney—it's a free template she must have downloaded online."

"Got it," the detective said. "We have Hilda's laptop at the lab for forensic analysis, but the techs haven't cracked her login credentials yet."

"Everything's left to the Ratzingers, including Rex," Tom continued.

Derek parsed the document before he let out a long, low whistle. "I'm afraid this complicates things for Dave."

Pete felt vindicated. "My position, exactly."

Kathy shook her head. "You'll never convince Rex."

"I'm with Kathy," Suzanne said. "We also found this on the ground in that stand of trees out back." She handed the prayer card over to Derek.

"Why would she—"

"Lose something so precious?" Kathy said. "We wondered that too. She must have been distracted the day she lost it. We're lucky that the wet weather didn't destroy it."

"We're still sorting through the photos," Suzanne said. "Our plan is to haul them home and keep working. But the boys discovered something else."

"Oh, yeah? Tell me."

"Well," Tom said, "Mrs. Wyndham left behind some interesting handwritten notes. The initials of a visitor she seems to have expected on Christmas Eve morning at six a.m. are 'D.R.'"

Dead quiet. Seconds passed.

"Dave is our number-one suspect now, isn't he?" Suzanne asked quietly.

Derek ran his fingers through his red hair. "He is. But everybody's a suspect until they're not. His wife claims he never moved from the house that morning. But now, with the Ratzingers being the beneficiaries of everything she owned, and then this, well— Can I see the notes?"

Tom produced the yellow pad, flipped to the correct page, and handed it to Derek.

"Good for you guys. Somehow, we missed these. Where did you find them?"

"The notepad was in a kitchen drawer," Tom said. "It's an easy miss. She buried it at the bottom of a heap of other bits of paper, and the note is the last thing she wrote on it."

"It doesn't look good, does it?" Pete said.

"It does not."

"Jump back a few pages," Tom prompted, "and you'll see a similar note with 'D.R.' That's the date Dave installed her new cupboards, just as he told us."

The detective skipped back to the right page. "Okay. I see it."

"Then there's the Bible verse," Kathy said softly.

"The what?"

"This was in the library, tucked into a book." She handed the three-by-five recipe card to Derek.

"It's written down in the yellow pad too," Tom said. "From Ezekiel 18:31."

Derek read the verse aloud: "'Cast away all the crimes you have committed, and make for yourselves a new heart and a new spirit! Why should you die…?'"

"So we were right," Kathy said.

"Right?" Derek asked.

"Yup. Hilda Wyndham had a secret. She was hiding something from the past—"

Pete couldn't contain himself. "Or hiding *from* something or someone *in* her past!" He rubbed his hands together.

"Whatever that secret was," the detective surmised, "I bet it'll lead us straight to the perpetrator."

10

AN UNEXPECTED VISITOR

At 2:03 a.m. on Saturday, Tom's cell phone buzzed, waking him from a foggy sleep. His first thought was, *I'm dreaming, right?* He sat up in bed, trying to figure out where the sound was coming from. Then it hit him.

His cell sat on the bedstand emitting an intermittent buzz. He picked it up: Unknown Caller, the screen read. He touched it. "Hello."

"Tom, it's me, Jack," a voice whispered.

"Jack . . ."

"Yeah, yeah, Jack Watson. You remember me, right?"

"Oh, sure, Jack. Uh-huh . . . I, uh . . . What time is it?"

"It's two in the morning. Tom, there's someone out here."

"Out where?"

"*Here.* At Mrs. Wyndham's house." His volume dropped even lower. "*Someone's in there.*"

"*What?* At two in the morning?"

"Yup."

"How do you know?" Tom asked as he jumped out of bed.

"Flashlight. Somebody's in the back bedroom where the library is. Every so often a beam of light flashes across the windowpane. *There . . . just did it again."*

Now wide awake, Tom raced across the hallway and shook his sister awake. "Is there a car parked out front?"

"Nope."

"You sure?"

"What's going on?" Suzanne asked groggily, sitting up.

"I don't see a car," Jack replied, "unless they parked on the other side of the house."

"Jack, stay where you are and watch what happens. Whatever you do, *don't go over there!* We're on our way—should be there in twenty minutes. Are your parents awake?"

"No way," he whispered even more softly.

The twins dressed quickly and jumped into the Chevy, Tom at the wheel. They hustled out to Highway 89.

"I'll text Kathy," Suzanne said. She tapped out a message: *Jack Watson called Tom—someone's inside Hilda's house. On our way.* She hit Send. No reply.

"And Derek," Tom said.

"You have his number?"

Tom groaned. "Yeah, back at the house. I didn't put it in my phone yet. Darn."

There was little traffic on 89. Two SUVs passed them, headed into the city. Then one semi, lit up like a Christmas tree, rushed past, followed by a motorcycle.

Twenty minutes later, the twins pulled up slowly—with the Chevy's lights doused—and parked just before the turnoff into Hilda's driveway. Darkness pervaded the entire house: no sign of life.

Across the street and one lot to the west, interior and exterior lights burned brightly from a long, low ranch-style home. Two figures emerged from the darkness, barely silhouetted by the distant light, hurrying toward them along the lane.

"Who's that?" Suzanne asked warily as the twins climbed out of their car.

"One of them is Jack, I'd guess. The other one must be his father."

That was the right call. Mr. Watson turned out to be a heavy-set guy, a little gruff but most interested in what had just occurred at Hilda's house.

An excited Jack whispered hoarsely, "We saw a shadow walk out the front door, didn't we, Dad?"

"We sure did," his father replied.

The twins shook hands with Mr. Watson and introduced themselves.

"Call me Hal," the man said. "Jack woke me up after he called you guys. It's so dark out here, we couldn't see much, but it was a man for sure."

"You didn't see a vehicle?" Tom asked.

Hal shook his head. "Nope. He just plain disappeared."

Jack raced ahead and tried the front door. "It's locked."

"We locked both doors on the way out yesterday," Suzanne said.

"How'd he get in?" Jack asked.

"Maybe he broke a window," Hal suggested.

The four of them circled the house, checking every window—no broken glass—and the back door. Locked.

"You know what that means?" Jack asked.

Suzanne glanced at him. "What's that?"

"The bad guy's got keys!"

Tom shook his head in frustration. "That makes things worse. How do you think that's possible?"

"Well," Jack said, "Dave's got a key."

"Why?"

"I dunno."

Suzanne unlocked the front door and the four trooped in. Tom flipped on lights in the living room, kitchen, and hallway as Jack raced toward the bedrooms.

"Nobody here!" he yelled out.

They crowded into the tiny library. Tom asked. "Anything different, Suzie?"

Seconds slipped by as Suzanne looked over the stacks of books she and Kathy had extracted from the shelve, one to the left, a second to the right. Next, she focused on the bookshelves, running her gaze across the rows. "Well, we never replaced a book upside down. Whoever was here did, with *three* books." She touched each of them with one finger.

Hal said, "So what?"

The twins eyed each other. "Are you thinking what I'm thinking?" Tom asked.

"I sure am. He's looking for the photos—or the will—or something else we haven't found yet." She turned to the Watsons. "One book was a simulated book, a box with a front cover that opened. Inside, we found tons of old photos, and Hilda's will. The Sheriff's Office has the will, and we've got the photos at home—it'll take us a bit to go through them."

"Oh, I get it," Hal said.

"Me too," Jack said, his face blazing with excitement.

"Just the fact that Hilda went to such lengths to conceal the photos and her will suggests that she was afraid of someone trying to find them," Tom said.

"Betcha anything he's in one of those photos!" Jack piped up again.

Suzanne couldn't help liking the little guy. For someone who wasn't even five feet tall yet, he was super sharp. "That makes perfect sense. He suspects or knows the cache exists, and he wants to make sure no one else finds it—."

"Too late for that," Tom quipped.

"True, but he can't know that," Suzanne said. "Not for sure, anyway."

Hal rubbed his chin. "Which means he might be back."

"You bet," Tom replied. "And if so, we'll be ready for him. We'll install a web-enabled camera in here. If he returns, we'll get a pic or two of this mysterious shadow, whoever he is."

Something occurred to Suzanne. "Jack, how did you spot him? I mean, what were you doing up in the middle of the night?"

Jack shrugged his shoulders. "Well, you guys asked me to keep a watch on Mrs. Wyndham's place. So I set my cell phone alarm to wake me every two hours, starting at midnight. You know . . . just in case."

THAT SAME MORNING, AT TEN O'CLOCK, THE BRUNELLIS— disappointed that they had missed Suzanne's text in the middle of the night—picked up the bleary-eyed twins. Pete grumbled all the way downtown. Soon, the mystery searchers trooped into the Sheriff's Office to meet with Detective Robinson.

A desk officer led them into a large meeting room with plenty of room to spread out. Derek sat at the head of the conference table with a file folder resting in front of him. "Come on in and make yourselves comfortable." He flipped open the file that lay before him. "Remember Burt Moore?"

"Sure, the guy across the lane," Pete replied.

"It turns out Burt served time in Colorado State Prison—five years for armed robbery. That kind of explains his prickly personality around a police officer."

"How long ago?" Kathy asked.

"Forty years."

"That puts him square on the suspect list," Tom noted.

"Well, it's possible. Anything's possible."

"What about Dave?" Suzanne quizzed.

"Clean as a whistle."

"And their wives?" Kathy asked.

"Nothing."

The mystery searchers brought the detective up to date, starting with the early-morning adventure, how the intruder had a key, and so did Dave, and the upside-down books.

"Sorry we couldn't call you," Tom said. "My fault—I left your phone number at home."

Derek chuckled. "No problem. Seems you did okay without my help. I've already had a few sleepless nights this month." He paused a few seconds and rubbed his square jaw. "So the intruder has keys and poked around in the library before disappearing into the dark. But the Watsons never spotted a vehicle—"

"That points to someone living on Sidewinder Lane," Kathy said.

"That points to Dave," Pete maintained. "I can't imagine it being anyone else. Sidewinder Lane is the last stop on the way to nowhere."

"You're being overly dramatic," his sister chided. "We'll go through the rest of the photos today. I'll bet anything they'll tell a story that the perp doesn't want told."

"Whoever he is, he couldn't find those pics—if that's what he's looking for," Tom explained to the detective, "so we figure he'll be back. While the girls are going through the photos, Pete and I will install a web-enabled video camera inside the house. It comes with a motion detector—if the guy passes within twenty feet of the wide-angle lens, the camera will capture images and forward them to my cell phone."

Detective Robinson's freckled face lit up in surprise. "Well, that's cool enough. You have a camera like that?"

"It belongs to our high school technology club," Pete replied. "We've used it on previous cases. The camera and motion detector install in less than an hour."

"I like it," Derek said, nodding in approval. "Anything new on Hilda's secret?"

"Not yet," Tom said.

"If we can ferret out the 'crime,'" Suzanne said, "we might have a good idea of who shut her up."

"'Shut her up?'" Derek echoed.

"Yes," Suzanne said. "That Bible verse really was a cry for help from a guilty conscience. I'll bet anything she wanted to resolve a crime in her past. But the guy who poured the poison didn't agree. He wanted her to keep the secret—forever."

"He didn't want exposure," Tom added.

"Go figure," Pete exclaimed. "Whatever the crime was, it had to be big. I'll bet there was a lot of money involved."

"One thing to be aware of," Derek advised, "is the statute of limitations. It slams into most—but not all—crimes. If a certain crime was committed more than seven years in the past, we can't charge someone with anything. That's the law in Arizona."

"That stinks," Suzanne said. She had a strong sense of justice.

"The perpetrator's gotta know that," Pete said. "He can't be that dumb."

"Something else too," Kathy said. "Her friend from the past had figured out what was in her mind. He came prepared."

"He sure did," Derek said.

"Prepared to bump her off," Pete said. "But whatever he said to Hilda did the trick instead."

11

CLUES

On Saturday afternoon, the foursome split into teams. While the boys drove off to pick up the camera system at Ray Huntley's ranch, Suzanne and Kathy combed through the photos on the Jacksons' dining room table.

Sherri sat down to help. "I love old pictures."

"Let's separate them into piles," Kathy suggested. "One for Wyndham family shots we can identify—Hilda, Troy, and Robert. Another for images of the Wyndhams with unidentified people. And a third for pics of Robert with his friends."

"Got it," Sherri said. She took over all the family photos.

"That leaves a few dozen images that include unknown people," Suzanne said. "We'll sort the 'unknowns' into groups. If an individual appears more than once, we'll pile those pictures together."

The fake book-box was deep and had hidden about two hundred prints. Time whipped by as the trio commented on each shot. "We'll never finish if we don't stop talking about them," Kathy nudged.

An hour later, they had ended up with eleven small stacks of shots of unknown people who appeared in multiple pictures. A few of the stacks featured people who were clearly relatives—Troy appeared to have three brothers, and they all had certain features in common that stood out. For example, they all started off as slim young men with blond hair but ended up looking a lot like Troy: with little or no hair. And they all gained considerable weight in their later years.

Hilda had two lady friends and they could have been sisters. Over the years the three appeared in nineteen photos: playing cards, sharing birthdays, and picnicking in summer grass or at the oasis.

Most images centered on Robert—a lot of elementary school pics paired him with friends. Robert liked sports, including football, but baseball stood out. Some shots displayed a pitcher surrounded by his teammates, accepting trophies, shaking hands with coaches, winning. Grinning. Laughing.

"You see that coach?" Kathy asked, holding up a photo of a bald, middle-aged man wearing a jersey. "I recognize him. His picture hangs in the main hallway at school."

The years slipped past as dozens of teenage color pics testified. One showed Robert proudly standing beside a classic two-door Dodge, with a friend beside him.

"His first car, I bet," Suzanne said. "Check it out. I've never seen one like that."

His buddy leaned across the car's long hood: a tall boy with dark hair and a slim build, looking relaxed, with an engaging face. Whoever that person was, he showed up in a handful of other photographs with Robert too.

There were other friends too. A redhead showed up in six shots —"A girlfriend, I'd guess," Sherri said.

Then a mysterious photograph, taken from the shore of a small pond, emerged from the depths of the book-box. Two boys—a little bit older now—were floating on inner tubes. Robert's face, frozen in laughter, was turned to the camera. His friend, with light-brown hair, peeked out from behind a hand that covered his face, with only his chin jutting out.

Something about the photo struck Kathy funny. Somehow the boy didn't look as if he was just horsing around. "That's odd," she said. "It's like he's *hiding*—like he *really* doesn't want his face in the photograph."

"Is that the pond in the oasis?" Suzanne asked. The girls had yet to visit the site for a closer look.

"It would make sense," Kathy replied.

Sherri dug through the family pics and found a few more of Robert with family. They scanned through the images one by one, checking for notations on the back. Nothing. They stopped and looked at one another.

"Okay, that's all of them," Suzanne announced.

"What's your plan now?" Sherri asked.

"Well—" Suzanne said. "Robert's girlfriend—if she's still around—she'd be in her sixties, right?"

"I guess so," Kathy replied. "We don't know Robert's date of birth, but it looks like Hilda had him when she was around maybe twenty-five."

"Let's find her. She could tell us about Robert. Like who his friends were, for example."

"Oh, I get it," Sherri said. "You're thinking about the young guy in the pond."

"Uh-huh. Hiding his face could be innocent, but you never know. And we need to find his buddy in the car photo too."

"How?"

"Yearbooks," Suzanne said. "The girlfriend and car buddy should be easy to find. Maybe one of them knows who the other guy is."

"Great idea." Kathy perked right up. "Prescott Library has got every Prescott High yearbook dating back to the 1920s."

"Let's go."

MEANWHILE, TOM AND PETE CRUISED OUT TO RAY HUNTLEY'S RANCH to pick up the camera system. Oddly enough, Ray lived north on 89, not ten miles from Hilda Wyndham's property.

Thirty minutes later, the boys pulled onto Hilda's driveway and parked. Pete grabbed the camera case from the backseat, and the two headed for the front door.

Someone yelled, "Hey, guys!"

They turned to see Jack dashing up the lane toward them with Rex in the lead. The dog sprinted over and greeted the boys.

"Hi, Jack!" the boys called out as they petted the friendly beast.

"Howdy. What's happening?"

The boys glanced at one another. "We're setting up some technology," Tom said. "But it's a secret."

Pete said, "You can't tell a soul."

"You can count on me."

Tom unlocked the front door and, as usual, Rex rushed in and flopped down on the kitchen floor in front of the fridge. The boys removed the camera from its small aluminum case and prepared to set it up, searching for a suitable hiding spot. Meanwhile, they explained the camera's purpose.

Jack loved every minute of it. "This is great," he said. More than once, too. "Is the suspect coming back tonight?"

"Who knows?" Tom replied. "We suspect he's after Hilda's family photos, or maybe some hidden papers but you never know."

The boys toured the house, debating where best to install the camera. Tom argued that the shot from inside the bookcase in the living room offered an unobstructed view of the front door and would give the best chance of capturing an intruder's face. Pete countered that if the intruder ransacked the bookcase, he'd surely find and destroy or steal the camera.

Tom won: an hour later the camera was stashed in the top shelf of the living room bookcase, nestled between two old books on Russian history. Tom recalled seeing a pad of colored construction paper in a kitchen drawer. He folded a sheet of black paper into the shape of a hardback book jacket that extended above the height of the camera, then pierced a small hole in it with a pushpin and aligned the aperture carefully with the lens and the electric eye. Pete attached the mock-up to the books on either side with tape, effectively disguising the camera as just another book.

"How do you know he'll use the front door?" Jack asked.

"There's an inside bolt on the back door," Pete replied. "I've already slid it closed. He locked the front door behind himself last time, so he must have that key. And now it's the only way in."

The boys ran a couple of tests using Jack as a stand-in for an intruder. He stepped outside, then crept through the front door. The camera went to work silently; less than a minute later, the image appeared on Tom's cell phone.

"We can set it to capture still or video images," Tom explained, showing Jack the still shot. "Stills upload faster."

"Cool!" Jack declared, laughing at his own picture. "This is serious detective stuff!"

1 2

THE HUNT CONTINUES

Suzanne and Kathy drove downtown, parking on Goodwin Street before strolling through the double doors of the library. Based on their guess at his age when he died, they had figured out the approximate years Robert would have attended Prescott High. Lorraine, a friendly librarian with steel grey hair, steered them into the right section. The girls removed the photos from a manilla envelope and set them on a table in front of them. They poured through their high school's ancient yearbooks. It didn't take long.

"Got him!" Kathy whispered with a flourish of excitement. "Here's his freshman year."

Suzanne glanced up from the yearbook she was perusing. "Oh, for sure. It's Robert. So that means—"

"That you've got his sophomore year."

"Yes. And here he is."

For the next hour they scoured through Robert's four years at Prescott High. With his interest in sports, Robert showed up in multiple images. He had worked on the school newspaper too.

Robert's car buddy surfaced early in their freshman year. The girls instantly recognized him: Billy Halliday was his name—same build, same face. He appeared often as the years slipped past.

But no one resembled anything like the young man in the oasis, His jutting jaw failed to show.

Then, in Robert's senior year, a girl named Rita Kellim appeared for the first time. "The girlfriend," Kathy said. "She must have transferred in." Rita was petite, with red hair and eyes that sparkled.

"That's her, all right," Suzanne said. "Let's hope she's still around."

"What now?"

"Well, I expect Rita would have married ages ago. We need to research online and at city hall, see if we can figure out her married name."

"In that case," Kathy prompted, "let's start with Billy Halliday." She Googled the name on her cell phone, adding '+ Prescott' to the search. "*Bingo.* Here he is."

"You're kidding. Here in town?"

"Yup. He lives on Overton Street, not a mile away."

AFTER INSTALLING AND TESTING THE CAMERA, TOM AND PETE trekked out to each of the ten homes that bordered Sidewinder Lane.

First up was Burt Moore's. "Whadaya want?" he barked at them as he opened his front door.

"We're working with Detective Derek Robinson," Tom replied in a calm voice. "I'm Tom Jackson and—"

"I'm Pete Brunelli." Pete stepped up and held his hand out.

"Whatever you're selling, I'm not interested," the man said, his face bunched up and creased by what looked like a permanent frown. He slammed the door shut. *Bang!*

"Man, oh man," Tom exclaimed. "So much for that conversation."

Pete stifled a laugh. "Bet anything he didn't treat Detective Robinson *quite* that way."

After their visit to Moore's place, Jack and Rex joined in the fun as the boys worked their way up and down the lane. That worked out fine—the boy knew everybody.

A newly married couple had only just moved into the last house at the western end of the lane. "My husband is at work," Lynn Whitewood explained. "But we heard all about Mrs. Wyndham's untimely death. To be honest, it scared us a little. My husband installed a security camera, just in case."

"Let us know if your camera captures anything suspicious," Tom said. She jotted down his phone number—just in case.

They met Dave's wife, Sarah, for the first time. "We're still—heartbroken," she said. "Such a tragedy and so unnecessary. I keep asking myself, why? But there is no answer, is there?"

"Not yet," Dave said, frowning. "But you mystery searchers will find an answer, won't you?"

One talkative retiree explained the genesis of Sidewinder Lane. "At one time this was the main road into Sidewinder Ranch. A guy named Krause homesteaded it a century ago. It's said that he spotted his first snake while building the family house, and it turned out to be a sidewinder."

Then he glared at the boys with one eye. "We might have another one running around, right, boys? The one responsible for whatever happened to Hilda."

In the end, no one had anything helpful to contribute to solving the case.

KATHY PULLED UP IN FRONT OF 34 OVERTON STREET AND PARKED THE Mustang. Suzanne grabbed the large manila envelope before the girls jumped out of the car and surveyed their destination: a two-story Victorian, just west of the county courthouse.

A sidewalk gate squealed as they pushed it open and walked up a narrow path. The stately home featured a wide wraparound veran-dah, three steps up. Suzanne rang the doorbell.

They heard footsteps before the inside door opened. A tall

gentleman looking to be in his sixties, thin with sparse hair and a ready smile, appeared. He held a newspaper in one hand. "Hello," he said warmly. "Can I help you?"

"We're looking for Mr. Billy Halliday," Kathy said.

The man chuckled. "Well, it's been a long time since someone called me Billy. But that would be me—Bill." He pushed open the screen door. "What can I do for you?"

Minutes later, the girls found themselves sitting side by side on an old-fashioned sofa in the formal living room. Bill sat across from them on an easy chair. Bill's wife—petite with pure white hair and eyes that hadn't lost their sparkle—served tea and biscuits. "Can I get you anything else?"

"No, no, we're fine. Thank you, Mrs. Halliday."

"Please, you don't have to be so formal. Call me Rita."

"Rita?" The girls gave each other a look.

"Yes."

"Your maiden name wouldn't have been Kellim?" Suzanne asked.

"Why, yes, it sure was." A look of astonishment crossed the woman's face. "How on earth did you know that?"

"What's this all about?" Bill asked.

"Do you both remember Robert Wyndham?" Kathy asked.

"Oh, sure," Bill replied, his face lighting up. "We were close friends in high school."

"I dated him for a few months in my senior year," Rita recalled. Her face said that the memory was a pleasant one. "You know he died many years ago . . . at a young age. Such a shame. His obituary appeared in *The Daily Pilot.*"

A coffee table anchored the center of the living room. Suzanne stood and slipped photos out of the manilla envelope, spreading three images apart on the table. The couple got to their feet and peered down at them.

"Oh, my goodness," Rita exclaimed. "There I am. I haven't seen that picture forever. I was so young."

"And beautiful," Bill said. "And you still are, darling." He gestured toward the second photo. "I remember that day as if it was yesterday. Robert's mother took that photo to celebrate his first car. He was so proud of it. Mrs. Wyndham was a wonderful woman."

"She just died a couple weeks ago," Rita said, pursing her lips, "under suspicious circumstances. We read about that in the *Pilot* too. So sad."

"That's why we're here," Kathy said.

"What do you mean?" Bill asked.

The girls explained, leading the Hallidays up to the third photograph. "We think it's possible this image is one of the things that the intruder was searching for," Kathy said, pointing to the young man floating with Robert in the pond.

"Do you recognize this person?" Suzanne asked.

The couple stared down at the photo. Seconds passed.

"I don't," Rita said, glancing at her husband. "Do you?"

"I—I'm not sure. I recognize the place, the pond out back at Robert's house. There's something vaguely familiar about the boy. But that hand in front of the face . . ." He hesitated. "You know, that was close to half a century ago."

A few minutes later, the girls said their goodbyes and headed out to the Mustang.

"Dead end," Suzanne groused.

"Yeah, maybe" Kathy replied. "But I still want to know who that boy is. I know it's just a hunch. But somebody might recognize him."

13

THE POND

"*He's back,*" Jack whispered urgently. "He's out here, again."

Tom sat bolt upright in his bed and glanced at his screen: Sunday, 2:34 a.m. "Jack, there's no way. The camera hasn't been triggered."

"That's because he's not in the house," Jack said.

"What do you mean?"

"Well, right now he's somewhere around the pond."

Tom raced across the hall to shake Suzanne awake, putting his phone on speaker so she could listen in. "The pond! What the heck's he doing there?"

"I dunno. But that's where the light beams are coming from. He doesn't realize it, but he's lighting up the top of those cottonwoods. I'm gonna wake up Dad."

"All right. But stay away from the guy—both of you. Keep a sharp eye open, see if you can tell where he disappears to—and how. We're on the way."

"Ten-four." *Click.*

Tom slipped back into his bedroom and pulled on his pants, smiling to himself. *Someday that kid will make an outstanding detective.*

Soon the twins were on 89, heading north with Suzanne at the wheel. Tom messaged Derek and the Brunellis. Two identical replies streamed back: *On the way.*

There was little traffic in either direction. One semi roared by them, on its way to Prescott, soon followed by a four-door sedan. And a motorcycle. Five minutes later, Suzanne spotted flashing blue lights in her rearview mirror.

"I'll bet that's Derek coming up behind us," she said.

Tom turned around and watched a sedan gain on them, blue lights flashing out front. "Whoa, he's moving fast." Seconds passed before the unmarked police vehicle cruised by at high speed. "He'll beat us out there."

"Not by much," Suzanne said. Two minutes later, she cranked hard onto Sidewinder Lane and soon pulled in behind Derek's parked car. He was standing next to the Watsons, in earnest conversation with Jack's dad.

Jack rushed over as the twins jumped out of the car. "He's gone," the boy said breathlessly. "We figure ten minutes ago."

"Did you see him leave?" Suzanne asked.

"Nope. The flashlight turned off and he flat-out disappeared."

"No vehicle?"

"Nope. And Dad and I were watching hard."

Derek and Hal Watson walked over to greet the twins. "I guess we missed him," Derek said. "Too bad."

"The weird thing," Hal said, "is we didn't spot the guy leaving. His flashlight lit up those cottonwoods. And then—gone."

"He never walked out front?"

"Nope."

"Let's look out there," Derek said.

They trooped behind one another, single file, with Derek leading. He held a large lantern-type flashlight in one hand, lighting the path all the way out. The group slipped through the cottonwoods and edged up to the pond.

"Check it out," Tom said. "The ground's wet here by the shore. Footprints in the mud. The guy was in the water."

"Oh, boy," Pete said, rubbing his hands together. "There's gotta be something in there."

"Or there *was* something in there," Kathy corrected him. "Whatever it was could be gone now. Maybe he found what he was looking for."

"Found what?" Suzanne asked.

"Evidence," Tom said. "He's trying to make something disappear."

"Look," Kathy said. "More footprints here in the dirt."

"Sure enough," Derek agreed.

A pathway led away from the pond, between the cottonwoods on the other side and east to the open field. Tom clicked on his cellphone flashlight and painted a path of light following the prints, but they soon vanished. The rough high desert floor made it impossible to track anything.

"Whoever this guy is," Pete said, "he walks right in and makes himself at home. He has a key to the house, he wades into the pond, and knows his way in and out of here."

"Which proves what?" his sister challenged.

"Which proves he lives close by," Pete said, lowering his voice. "Maybe even next door."

"Problem with that hypothesis," Derek said pointedly, "is that he walked east, not west."

"Meaning. . .?" Kathy asked.

"Dave's house is to the west," Suzanne said, "and it's dark as the ace of spades."

"So noted," Pete said.

"What now?" Kathy asked.

"We go for a swim," Tom said with a laugh.

1 4

A RUSTY CLUE

On Sunday after church, the Jackson and Brunelli families enjoyed brunch at their favorite Mexican restaurant. On the menu were Pete's favorites, spicy-hot tamales and delicious cheese enchiladas.

"*Mmm-mmm,*" he said, finishing off his second bowl of taco chips. "We need more salsa."

"There's mild, medium, hot, and wretched," Tom said, grinning. "You're polishing off the wretched variety."

"Bring it on."

LATER, THE MYSTERY SEARCHERS HEADED BACK TO HILDA'S HOME. Pete was at the wheel of their hot Mustang, and the Jacksons occupied the backseat.

According to Pete, it was a perfect day for a dip in the pond.

"You know, you really are nuts," his sister commented along the way. "That water will be ice-cold. In fact, we're lucky that it's not frozen solid."

"A bracing swim," Pete teased. "And I'll be the first one in."

"After eating like that, you'll probably sink like a rock."

"I might beat you in," Tom said. "It's all about attitude."

Suzanne recalled a swim from the past. "Kathy, you didn't like the swamp in Skull Valley either, remember? But we all jumped in."

"Eeww," Kathy replied, wrinkling her nose. "Tom said you can't even see the bottom of this pond."

Tom fessed up. "Yeah, but the water won't hurt you."

Pete bugged, "Unless you freeze to death."

Soon, Pete nosed the car into Hilda's gravel driveway and pulled to a stop.

"Here comes Jack," Tom said. "And Rex. Check it out. The kid's got his bathing suit on—and no towel!"

Pete grinned. "Maybe I won't be first."

"Nothing gets past that boy," Kathy said. She grabbed towels from the backseat and climbed out. Tom slipped a flashlight, enclosed in a plastic ziplock bag, into his jean jacket pocket. All four had bathing suits on under their clothes.

Jack couldn't have been more excited if he tried. "Let's go!" He leapfrogged past the foursome, right behind Rex, circled the house and raced along the path through the cottonwoods. He jumped into the water—*splash!*—and disappeared below the surface.

"He's stirring up the mud," Kathy complained. "It's disgusting— and bad for visibility too."

"You big chicken," her brother teased. "Gimme that flashlight, Tom." He dropped his clothes and slipped down into the water, careful not to agitate the silty bottom further. *"Yikes!* It really drops off fast."

Then, nothing. Seconds later, the two broke the surface and gasped for breath before dropping back down, three times in total. Then they gave up and pulled themselves out.

"This is fun!" cried Jack.

"The water's about five feet deep," Pete said between gulps of air. "Nothing down there but rocks and mud. And it's *freezing.*"

"Told 'ya."

"Who's next?" Tom asked.

"C'mon, Kathy," Suzanne begged. "We swam out at Skull Valley. You can do it."

Kathy blanched. "Sure, but the water wasn't freezing." But she gave in grudgingly. "You first. Give me the flashlight, Pete."

The two girls waited a bit for the water to clear, then squealed and glided into the pond, disappearing beneath the surface. They popped up twice for air, then slipped down again. A minute passed before they shot up once more.

"I got it!" Kathy cried out in triumph. She made her way to the edge and climbed out with a hand from Pete. Suzanne was right behind her.

"What?" her brother demanded, handing her a towel. "You got what?"

"Patience." She pulled herself out to her feet, shivering and half frozen. Her lips had turned blue and her teeth chattered. "I've never been so cold in my life." She wrapped herself up in a towel.

"What is it, Kathy?" Suzanne shouted. "What did you find?"

Kathy held out her hand. "These!" A rusty set of car keys appeared—two keys, heavily corroded, attached to an encrusted metal keyring. "This is what he was looking for—and didn't find."

"Just lying there, on the bottom?" Tom asked.

"Nope. Stuck between two rocks. I didn't see it until Suzie pushed a rock aside. The keys dropped right into my hand."

Suzanne gave her a high-five. "Whoo-hoo!"

"Who owned them?" Jack asked.

"No clue—yet," Tom replied. "It's my turn. There could be something else down there." He grabbed the ziplock-clad flashlight and slid into the pond. After a couple of dives, he surrendered and climbed out.

"The keys must have been the number one item on the perp's bucket list," Pete figured. "There's nothing else down there."

"At least nothing we've found," Tom added. Like the others, he had pulled his clothes back on and zipped up his jacket.

"Where did Rex go?" Suzanne asked, looking around.

"Aw, he's just wondering around," Jack replied. "He does that all the time."

Soon the group headed out of the cottonwoods and back toward the house. They spotted Rex, sitting a few hundred yards south—past Hilda's property and over the service road—on federal government land. Jack whistled. The dog sprang to his feet and sprinted over.

"Boy, that dog is well trained," Pete said.

Suzanne said, "Smart too."

LATER THAT AFTERNOON, THE MYSTERY SEARCHERS MET HEIDI AND Derek at the Shake Shack. "The Shack," their favorite meeting spot since junior high, featured outside picnic tables and delicious hamburgers and shakes. Even in cold weather, it was a nice place to sit.

The twins arrived first and skipped their usual shakes. "Too chilly for me," Suzanne said. "Let's get some coffee after everyone shows."

The Brunellis arrived minutes later. Derek drove in right behind Heidi. The two met for the first time.

"The sheriff loved your follow-up story on Hilda Wyndham," Derek said.

"Always happy to support our local constabulary," Heidi said. "Besides, that poor woman needs a little justice."

Tom slipped into the restaurant as the others brought Derek and Heidi up to date.

"Our perpetrator skipped the house this time," Kathy said, "and headed straight to the pond."

"Why would he do that?" Heidi asked.

"It's possible he figured the sheriff had already found whatever the perp was looking for inside—the photos or Hilda's will, we suspect," Suzanne explained. "Our hunch is, that could turn into a huge problem for him because of this image"—she laid a photo down on the table before them—"which shows Robert and a buddy floating in the pond."

"Could be the guy remembers this photo," Kathy said, picking up the theory, "and realizes it might lead to him—"

"And to the evidence in that pond," Pete interrupted.

"What evidence?" Derek asked in a flat voice.

"These," Kathy said, opening her hand. "We figure either this guy or Robert threw these keys in the pond back in the day."

"Which explains his early-morning swim," Suzanne said. "That evidence needed to disappear."

Tom returned with a tray of steaming hot coffee cups, cream, and sugar on the side. He passed the cups around.

Derek plucked the keys from Kathy's hand and scrutinized them slowly.

"Look closely," said Pete. "It's possible these are truck keys."

"What makes you think that?" Derek asked.

"GMC makes both cars and trucks. Hold the keys toward the sun and tilt them slightly."

"Right you are," said Derek. "I can make out the GMC symbol. Just barely."

"But what's their significance, that's what we need to know," Tom said.

"Whatever it is," the detective replied, "it's critical to the guy who decided on a freezing late-night swim. Somehow these keys must represent a serious threat to his future."

"How?" Heidi asked.

"They could lead us to a crime in the past," Tom said, ". . . to Hilda's secret."

"These keys fit a vehicle—or they did once," said Pete excitedly. He loved anything to do with cars. "How are we ever gonna find it?"

"Good question," the detective replied. "The vehicle might well not exist anymore."

"The perp thinks it's still around," Tom said. "Otherwise. . ."

"If it dates back to Robert's high-school days, it would be forty-some years old," Kathy argued. "Long gone."

"Can anyone identify Robert's pond buddy?" Heidi asked.

"Not yet," Suzanne said. "We tried." The girls described their visit to the Hallidays. "So far, it's a dead end."

"Can I borrow this pic?" Heidi asked.

"Oh, sure," Suzanne said. "What are you going to do with it?"

"Run it on the front page tomorrow morning."

TECHNOLOGY

Tom always did his best thinking late at night, after everyone else had gone to bed. He relaxed until midnight, watching an episode of his favorite old television series, *The Twilight Zone*, featuring three astronauts who returned to earth only to find that no one remembered them. *Well, that would be one way to escape from your past,* Tom thought.

Then he sat in the dark, quiet and still, brooding. *We're missing something. Something obvious. It's right in front of our faces. I can feel it. The guy realizes the sheriff is looking for him . . . and he's worried. Plenty worried.*

Tom recalled his father's words: *"What clues did the perpetrator leave behind? . . . . That could stir him into risky actions he wouldn't normally take."* Like hunting for the keys in the pond in the middle of the night. Bad move. Risky. Careless.

Tom reviewed the events of the case methodically: Finding Rex at Watson Lake . . . Hilda Wyndham's untimely death . . . Carfentanil and the coffee mug . . . the sheriff's quest for justice . . . Jack . . . "D.R." . . . Dave Ratzinger . . . and the rude guy across the street with a criminal record . . .

Next Tom mentally played back scenes of the house, room by

room: Hilda's notes. The Bible verse, copied twice. Rex on the kitchen floor, by the fridge. The library and the concealed cache of photos. Then outside: The barn and the empty garage. A digger and the tractor.

The fields and the pond. And the keys. *Wait! Stop.* Tom sat straight up.

The digger. *The digger.*

MONDAY MORNING'S EDITION OF *THE DAILY PILOT* FEATURED A TIGHT, cropped photo on the front page. A close-up of Robert's buddy appeared, one hand over his face, with a caption:

Do you know this man? The Yavapai County Sheriff's Office is seeking an individual considered to be a witness in an active investigation. This photograph could be more than forty years old. If you recognize this man from the past, please call the tip line at the Yavapai County Sheriff's Office.

"It's kind of a long shot," Suzanne said.

"A family member might recognize him," Tom said. "I mean, you can just see a little—the hair, the jutting chin."

"The best part about this picture," the Chief said, "is that he's on the front page. You're putting a lot of heat on the guy—if the perp and this photo really are connected."

"Yup. And he's reacting," Suzanne agreed. "A dip in the pond was a bad move on his part."

"You're not kidding," the Chief said.

"Dad, I've got an idea," Tom said.

"Uh-oh," his sister teased.

"No, I'm serious. Remember the mechanical digger, the one behind Hilda's barn?"

"You mentioned it," the Chief replied.

"Sure," Suzanne said, recalling the faded yellow Caterpillar..

"What's it for?"

"You said the property was once farmed," said the Chief. "So—digging up rocks to clear the fields?"

"Not likely," Tom said. "I think someone buried something out there."

"Like what?" asked Suzanne.

"Like—a—vehicle," Tom intoned.

"A vehicle!" Suzanne cried.

"The digger must have had a purpose."

"That hole would be enormous," she said doubtfully.

"That's the purpose of a digger."

The Chief dusted a crumb off his immaculate uniform. "Diggers wouldn't be common on properties like those."

"But think about it," Suzanne protested. "Even if you are right—ten acres—how would we ever figure out where something's buried?"

PRESCOTT HIGH'S TECHNOLOGY CLUB HAD SPENT THE PREVIOUS YEAR trying to adapt a magnetometer, a device that detects and measures magnetic fields, as a drone-enabled metal-detector. They had purchased off-the-shelf hardware to save money, cobbled the pieces together, and written their own software. But success had eluded the team so far. For one thing, the weight of the magnetometer, a heavy, ten-inch-long tube that hung under the drone, negatively affected lift and maneuverability. Commercial metal-detecting drones had much more powerful rotors.

"We only got lift of about four feet," Tom explained as the mystery searchers cruised north in the Chevy later that morning. "That doesn't work in many real-world situations, because of obstacles. But the only danger on Hilda's land are those cottonwoods; we'll work around them. Anyway, the closer to the ground the magnetometer is, the better it works."

The homemade software was another story. Not only was it

buggy, but the onscreen TIFF map images were often wrong. "That's been the biggest issue," Tom said. "False readings were common in our tests, but every so often they proved accurate. We knew it was in the coding, but ran out of time."

Suzanne pulled up to Ray's house at 10 a.m. that same morning. All four got out and chatted with the technology club's president on the front porch. They loaded the equipment into the Chevy's trunk —one aluminum case for the drone, another for a laptop and associated hardware.

"I charged it up after you called," Ray informed them. "You should have plenty of juice. What's happening?"

"Ever hear of Hilda Wyndham?" Suzanne asked.

"Oh, sure. She lived a few miles from here. We read about her in the newspaper. Her death was suspicious, right?"

"Right."

"So that's where the camera is?"

"Yup," Pete said. "Hidden in her house. We're hoping the perpetrator returns."

Ray nodded his approval. "Go get him."

Ten minutes later, Suzanne parked the Chevy Impala on Hilda's driveway and the foursome unloaded the two metal shipping cases. Jack popped right over with Rex.

"Hi, everyone!" he called out. "What's happening?"

Rex greeted the mystery searchers with sloppy kisses and tore far across the field on the south side of the house. . . out to his regular spot on the federal land.

Jack and Pete lugged the two cases out behind the barn. They set up right beside and inside the digger, using the floor of the cab as a stationary platform for the laptop.

"How's this going to work?" Kathy asked.

Tom explained as he powered up the system and programmed the drone to survey a target area of ten acres, whose boundaries he defined by placing dots around all four sides of the property on the map display. The drone would fly a parallel zigzag path while the magnetometer recorded anomalies in the earth's magnetic field, an indirect way of finding metal.

"This tubular device will generate a three-dimensional geolocated map of the area," Tom said. "It'll look like a heat map, but it measures magnetic fields, down to a depth of a hundred feet or so for really large metal objects—like buried cars, for example—when it works."

"How often is that?" Pete asked.

"Not often enough. Fifty-fifty at best. Is the drone ready, Suzie?"

"Ready!"

"Let 'er fly."

With a loud buzzing sound, the drone lifted to its maximum height, which—with the tubular device hanging beneath—was just over four feet. It crossed over to the east side of the property, traveling in a straight line south.

Everyone locked onto the laptop screen. "Check out that image," Kathy said.

Superimposed over a Google Earth–style photo of Hilda's property, the drone was gradually building a rainbow-hued image, strip by strip, that really did remind them of a heat map.

"If there are metal objects buried here, or deposits of magnetic minerals," Tom explained, "the map will look like mountainous terrain, with peaks and valleys. At least it's working. But all we're seeing so far is dirt."

The drone slogged its way back and forth from east to west as if plowing north-to-south furrows in the long-untilled fields, electronically blanketing every square foot of the property and displaying the results in real time. The foursome's focus shifted between the drone itself and the screen. But nothing unusual showed up. Anywhere.

After two complete passes over the entire acreage, Tom had had enough. "Let's just bring it home," he said.

The drone landed in the same spot it had taken off.

"Well, it was a great thought," Tom said, his face speaking volumes. "But—"

"Stay positive," his sister urged.

"Check out Rex," Pete said. "Look where he's lying down."

Kathy glanced over to the dog. "He's on the federal government land. So what?"

"He goes to the same spot every time. Why not try the drone out there?"

"Outside the property?" Tom asked.

"If you were a criminal," Pete replied, "wouldn't it be the dumbest thing ever to bury evidence on your very own land?"

"Point taken," Tom said, his spirits rising again.

Jack said, "Pete's right. Criminals aren't that stupid."

"Well, they often are, actually," Suzanne said. "But, Tom," she urged, "that makes perfect sense. Run it around the outside of the property. Hey, it's worth a try."

"Okay." Tom plotted changes on the map, instructing the drone to survey an additional fifty feet outside the property's boundaries on all four sides. Then he touched Go on the screen.

The drone rose again and traveled to the left, winging its way toward the federal government land bordering the Wyndhams'. After the little aircraft had finished on one side, it turned hard right. It had just passed over Rex—he barked at it—when Kathy shouted, "*Look!* Check out the screen."

There, at one corner of the image, instead of the spectrally colored, rippling little hills and troughs that covered Hilda's land, a bright-pink box-like shape emerged, like a miniature squared-off mesa.

"It's working!" Tom shouted. "There's something there. And it's huge!"

Jack shouted, *"You did it!"*

Pete whooped, "Rex showed us!"

Tom brought the drone home. Everyone crowded around the screen to examine the image as Tom rotated and zoomed in on it to view the magnetic anomaly they had discovered from varied perspectives.

"It's some kind of a vehicle, I think," Tom proclaimed.

Pete was so excited he could hardly stand it. He raced over to the tool shed, grabbed a shovel, and hustled across the land. The dog sat up as he approached. "What are you protecting, Rex? What's under there, buddy?"

The others followed and watched as Pete furiously chopped a hole in the high desert ground. He bored straight down as best he could—underneath a thin level of gritty cover, the land was hard, like solid clay. Just two feet down, his shovel hit something. Something hard. *Bang, bang.*

Pete grinned. "Tom, it's metal. Hard metal. Betcha anything it's the roof of a vehicle." He glanced over to his best friend before hammering it again. *Bang.* "You know what? You're a regular genius."

"Brilliant!" Suzanne agreed. She reached for her cell phone in her back pocket and tapped Derek's number.

16

DAYLIGHT

That afternoon at 2 p.m., Hilda Wyndham's driveway and Sidewinder Lane turned into a parking lot.

Sheriff McClennan and Detective Robinson pulled up in an unmarked cruiser and parked behind the Jacksons' Chevy. The Chief showed up five minutes later, just before a county wrecker rattled onto the driveway. The two senior officers greeted one another; they were lifelong friends, both born and raised in Prescott. For the first time, the Chief met County Detective Derek Robinson.

The sheriff directed the wrecker's driver. "Go around the cars!" he shouted, waving his arms, "and park behind the barn!" The huge recovery vehicle belched smelly diesel smoke into the air as it skirted the outbuildings. The girls plugged their noses.

Jack ran over with his father. "This is exciting! Nothing ever happens on Sidewinder Lane." Dave ambled over with Rex secured on a leash. The dog barked at the Chief, which amused the twins to no end.

"Rex is being Rex," Kathy quipped.

Suzanne had texted Heidi the previous evening. The star reporter arrived and parked in the lane. Next, a large van appeared with six county workers, each with a shovel. Their job was to clear off as much dirt as possible, enough to allow the wrecker access to the buried vehicle's front or rear bumper—if there really was an auto of some kind down there.

Minutes later, the sheriff called out, "We're ready! Lead on, Tom —the wrecker will follow you."

The mystery searchers trekked out to the end of the property, crossed the service road and onto federal land. Everyone else followed the enormous truck as it belched and bumped across the earth. Soon enough, Pete spotted the hole he had dug the previous afternoon. "Right here!" he yelled.

The six county workers walked over and began to dig. Within minutes, a flat, gunmetal-grey roof emerged from the past.

"That thing is huge," Suzanne said.

"It's driving me nuts," Pete griped impatiently. "I mean, why bury a—well, whatever it is? What's it doing under there?"

"Are we at the back of it?" Detective Robinson asked the county workers.

"It sure looks that way," one worker replied. "I think that's the start of a rear window."

"Okay. Focus there and dig down."

"Got it."

All eyes locked onto the surreal scene. "Your first guess was right, Pete," Tom said. "I think it's a truck."

Twenty minutes later, the workers had unearthed the rear window entirely. They continued digging their way deeper. Two back doors appeared. Then a bumper with a weathered license plate. Suzanne watched as the detective reached for his cell phone. *He's running the number.*

"That's all I need," the driver of the wrecker declared. "I'll pull a U-turn and back it up close. Everyone out of the way!"

The wrecker pulled a wide three-sixty and backed into place with an ear-piercing roar. The driver jumped out of the truck and grabbed the hook attached to a massive chain, dropping it into the freshly dug hole. Then he clamored down to the exposed bumper and latched the hook onto it

He climbed back up and into the driver's seat.

"Okay!" he bellowed. "Here she comes!"

The wrecker revved up with a roar, grinding gears and belching more smoke. The chain pulled taut with a tremendous clanking sound. The buried truck shuddered and then, ever so slowly, it growled its way out of the earth, one foot at a time, as mounds of dirt tumbled to the high-desert floor. The noise was deafening, the air hazy with a ghastly brew of dust and putrid smoke. Minutes later, the truck levitated fully into daylight and stopped.

"I can't believe it," Derek said. "It's—

"*An armored truck,*" Pete whooped. "Who could ever have—"

"Settle down," Kathy admonished him.

The sheriff shook his head. "And I thought I'd seen everything."

"Anyone recall an armored truck ever going missing around these parts?" the Chief asked.

"Nope," said the sheriff. "Interesting, isn't it?"

Kathy walked over to one side of the vehicle and chipped away some encrusted dirt. A rusty red logo appeared, letter by letter: LEWIS ARMORED SERVICE. And under that, FLAGSTAFF, ARIZONA. She looked over to the two senior officers. "Ever hear of them?"

"Never," the Chief said.

"Nope," the sheriff said. "Flagstaff's in Coconino County."

Heidi's camera clicked softly as she captured images from every angle, including close-ups of the graphics. "Holy doodle," she whispered, almost to herself.

"Your editor is gonna love this," Kathy said.

"Wait a minute," Suzanne said. "I have an idea."

"Go ahead," the sheriff said. "We're all ears."

"If this story gets out now officially—I mean, about finding this armored truck—our suspect, whoever he is, could pull a disappearing act. We're lucky he hasn't done that already. Why not let the local rumor mill run with it . . . Hilda's death is a big story, the whole town must already be talking about it. I mean, look—" She pointed toward the crowd of bystanders who had gathered in the road by the edge of Hilda's property. A dozen people or more were on their cell phones.

"Well, that's a fact," Derek said, chuckling.

The crowd was growing. It looked like almost all of Hilda's neighbors had streamed in from Sidewinder Lane, and some of them were shooting photos and videos. Two of the county workers were on their cells too.

"So your idea," the Chief summed up, "is to let the perp hear about the discovery as a rumor."

"Right," Suzanne said. "He might not want to believe it, if there's no coverage anywhere in local media. The Sheriff's Office would have to do a complete blackout—ask the *Pilot*"—she indicated Heidi, who smiled in response—"local TV, and radio all to hold off for now. That might force the perp to check it out for himself."

"Unless he's already here," Pete said, as he looked over the crowd. His eyes ticked over to Dave, then to where, at the back, behind everyone else, stood Burt Moore, arms folded, glowering.

"You guys think that's a possibility?" the Chief asked.

"It's a maybe," said Kathy.

"Heidi," the sheriff called out to the reporter, "you can keep this out of the paper, in print and online, for a couple days, right?"

"Right. Glad to. Two days. And there's no other media out here. You'd better hide that armored truck in the barn, though." Then she added, "Sightseers."

"You know," said Suzanne. "The best way to get people talking .. . is to ask them not to."

"Right you are, young lady," the sheriff said. He ordered the wrecker to turn off his noisy engine, then called out to the crowd, "Gather around, people! I've got an announcement to make." He waited while the neighbors edged closer. "I want everyone to listen to me, carefully. We need to put a pause in our investigation here—just for a couple of days. We're going to push this armored truck into the barn there"—he pointed to the empty red building—"and that's where the county crime scene unit will take over, soon."

Someone in the crowd shouted, "How come, Sheriff?"

"I can't say," he replied. "But this will help with the investigation." He paused for a few seconds to let his words sink in. "What I'm asking all of you to do is to keep this among ourselves for forty-eight hours. Then you can tell anybody you want."

"People are talking already," another voice piped up.

"We know," the sheriff replied. "We'll live with that."

AN HOUR PASSED BEFORE SIDEWINDER LANE EMPTIED. JACK AND HIS father headed home, much to the boy's displeasure. The mystery searchers and Heidi chatted with Detective Robinson and the Chief, waiting for the sheriff to complete an extended phone call.

"The crime scene investigators are on the way," Derek told the mystery searchers. "It'll be interesting to see what's in that truck." No one could enter the vehicle until the techs had completed their work.

"Suzie," the Chief said, "that was a great idea on your part. Everybody in Prescott will soon have learned about the buried armored truck. If that doesn't drive the perpetrator out here, nothing will."

A few minutes later, the sheriff disconnected. "That was Sheriff Rich Connor of Coconino County. He should be here within the hour. Someone hijacked that truck forty-five years ago."

Pete let out a long, low whistle. "Wow! Did they steal money?"

"One hundred and twenty-five thousand dollars," the sheriff replied gruff voice.

"*Sheesh,*" Kathy said. "That would have been serious money back then."

"It sure would have been," Derek said. "Where was it hijacked, Sheriff?"

"Sixty miles north of us. Williams, Arizona—right after you cross into Coconino County. That's why I never heard of the crime. Not only is Williams outside my jurisdiction, the hijacking occurred when I was in high school."

The Chief chortled. "Steve, I had no idea you were that old."

"This job would age anyone," the sheriff said with a wry smile.

"How did they pull it off?" Tom asked.

"An armored courier guy walked into an after-hours pickup location and never came out. They're called 'hoppers' because they hop from one site to another. When the hopper didn't return, the driver did something he shouldn't have: he left the truck and headed into the facility himself." He paused and grimaced. "Bad training. Real bad. Two guys with a handgun and Halloween masks had broken in—through the roof. They took both guards prisoner and locked them up in a walk-in safe. No one started looking for them for a couple hours; by then, the truck had disappeared . . . from the face of the earth."

"Literally!" said Kathy.

"To the best of our knowledge, Dave and Hilda never crossed paths four and a half decades ago," Tom reasoned. "I think we can cross Dave Ratzinger off the suspect list."

"I'm sure you're right," Derek said.

"So the case remained unsolved," Suzanne said.

"That's a fact," Heidi said. "No one ever saw the truck again—until today."

"But Hilda knew," Kathy said. "And it ate her alive."

"Which must," Tom concluded, "be why she's dead."

CLUES

S heriff Rich Connor made excellent time, cruising straight down Highway 89 to arrive in just in forty-five minutes. He pulled up on Sidewinder Lane and headed over to the open barn. Medium tall and trim with a brushed haircut and dressed in his khaki uniform, the imposing Coconino County sheriff shook hands with the other officers—they had all known each other for years—and met Detective Robinson for the first time.

The wrecker had long since returned to the city. Sheriff Connor examined the back end of the armored truck, still coated with dried mud, and shook his head in amazement. "When I took this job ten years ago, I learned about the hijacking as part of my orientation, in a review of unsolved cases. I never heard it mentioned again."

"It's the getaway lost in time," Tom said.

"That's an understatement," Suzanne said.

The Chief stepped up. "Rich, I'd like to introduce you to the mystery searchers. They located the buried truck using some home-made technology and excellent detective work."

The four shook hands with Sheriff Conner. Kathy dragged Heidi over and presented the star reporter.

"Pleased to meet all of you," Sheriff Conner said. "We subscribe to *The Daily Pilot* in my office, so I'm familiar with your track record. Great work."

Heidi and the mystery searchers smiled and thanked him.

The team of crime technicians had arrived and were busy chipping encrusted mud from the windows and doors. It wasn't long before one of them called out, "We're ready, Sheriff!"

"They're going into the vehicle now," Sheriff McClennan said. "Should be interesting."

The double back doors swung open, for the first time in forty-five years. An investigator dressed in a hooded white hazmat suit climbed up into the truck. With gloved hands, he picked up six cream-colored canvas money bags, one at a time, and turned them inside out. Empty. Then he held up two Halloween masks—Mickey and Minnie Mouse—and dropped them and the empty sacks into large, see-through plastic evidence bags.

Other crime scene techs, all dressed in identical protective clothing, opened the two side doors. One plucked a folded map from the right side of the dash, depositing it into another evidence bag. Two sets of rubber gloves had all but disintegrated on the truck's floor, but the technician meticulously scraped up the desiccated residue. Then . . . nothing. Still, over the following hour, the five investigators combed through the truck, dusting for prints, trying to collect dust and fibers.

Finally, the lead crime technician walked back to the assembled group. "You saw the items we retrieved. There's nothing else that stands out," she said. "We've checked for prints and microscopic evidence, but we're not expecting lab analysis to tell us much. Somewhere along the line, three feet of water flooded the truck, which caused extensive damage."

Tom asked, "Can we look at the map you found?"

The investigator glanced toward Sheriff McClennan for permission. "It's fragile," she warned.

"You handle it," he ordered.

She carefully removed the map from its evidence bag with gloved hands and opened it over the hood of Sheriff McClennan's car.

A thick red line traced a route from Williams to Prescott, through the back country.

"Yeah, I get it," Sheriff Conner said. "No wonder no one spotted the getaway."

"I'm not familiar with that route," Detective Robinson said.

"Not surprising," Sheriff Connor said, taking a deep breath. "Few people are. I had my office check on what happened the night of the hijacking. The records show that we had officers on Interstate 40, both sides of Williams. Neither of them spotted an armored truck that night, which at the time seemed odd. Now we know why."

"They took a little-used back trail," Pete said, bending closer.

"They sure did," Sheriff Connor said. "Look: the hijackers traveled south on Fourth Street out of Williams. That becomes the little-used Perkinsville Road, or County Road 73. It meanders a few miles through Kaibab National Forest, descending steeply all the way." He traced a finger along the red line, hovering over the map. "Real pretty drive, lined with pine trees, juniper, oak, and mesquite."

"You wouldn't notice that at night," Suzanne said.

"Nope," the sheriff continued. "Once you leave Coconino County and enter Yavapai County, the road becomes County Road 70. Two dozen miles later, the pavement ends, but the road is still suitable for a regular passenger vehicle—as long as the weather is good."

"This isn't a passenger car . . ." Pete said.

"You got that right," Sheriff McClennan replied. "I've been on this road. It's not for the faint-hearted. The bottom is a long way down."

"We all hiked it a couple years back," Kathy said. "All the way to the Verde River."

"Yeah, it's real pretty country," Sheriff Connor continued. "Then they'd turn right on County Road 72 and wind their way toward

Perkinsville—it's not a town, more like a ranch. They'd have to traverse the one-lane Perkinsville Bridge across your Verde River."

"That's right where we were hiking," Suzanne said. "There's a sign that points to Jerome, then the road turns into a winding, one-lane gravel road for the next few miles; it follows the old bed of the United Verde and Pacific Railway."

"Best part was, there's no guardrail to prevent cars from plummeting off the cliff," Pete said with a wicked grin.

"Says you," Kathy objected. "It freaked me out. One wrong step and you're history. Then Jerome appeared . . . you're looking down at the town—*way* down."

"Quite a trip," the Chief said. "After that, it's a thirty-five-mile jaunt to Prescott—which could've been the most dangerous part of the getaway."

"Why is that?" Tom asked.

"Because they'd be on Highway 89, with traffic," Sheriff Connor replied. "By then, there'd be an APB out for them. If a Department of Public Safety officer had spotted them, it might have been game over.."

"And an armored car is not exactly inconspicuous," Tom said.

LATER THAT EVENING, SUZANNE'S IDEA ABOUT USING GOSSIP TO DRAW the perp back to Hilda's home morphed into a workable plan of action. Tom flipped a coin and the Brunellis won. Or lost, depending on you looked at it.

"I hate all-nighters," Kathy groaned.

"You complain too much," her brother said. "I can't wait."

Pete figured the perp would show again. In his two previous forays onto Hilda's property, the suspect had made his appearance between 2:00 and 3:00 a.m.

"But there's no guarantee he'll stay on the same timeline," Pete reminded. "Kathy and I will shoot out at eleven o'clock tonight, and call it a night at four a.m."

Over a speakerphone call, Derek agreed to accompany them from midnight on. "If the guy doesn't show up by then, it's over."

"What are our chances?" Kathy asked.

"Who knows?" Derek replied. "It all depends on when he hears the rumor. If someone mentioned it to him today, he might show up tonight. If not . . ."

18

EARLY WARNING

W hen Kathy said she hated the all-nighters, she wasn't kidding. And this one looked to be the worst ever.

Hal Watson allowed them to park on his property. The last thing they wanted to do was alert the perp with the presence of a car. That suited Jack just fine.

"I'll be watching out for you," he said after they had parked the Mustang.

The siblings set up shop in the empty garage beside the barn. Pete had brought a space heater from home and placed it on the floor, right by their feet. The outside temperature dropped to the forties, and it seemed just as cold inside the garage. But the space heater quickly warmed the area to sixty-two degrees, which was, well, bearable.

"Can you crank it up?" Kathy asked. She was wearing jeans, a heavy sweatshirt, and a ski jacket rated for below zero. And gloves and a scarf. She still shivered.

"It's on maximum," Pete replied. "Quit whining. Any warmer and you'd die from the heat."

"Speak for yourself."

They rustled up three old barstools from the tool shed and set them before a window overlooking the rear of the property. That ensured a view straight back toward the government land.

"Minus the cottonwoods," Pete noted, "if a mouse moved, we'd see it."

"If the mouse had its own flashlight, maybe," Kathy quipped. She shook her head. When she surveyed the landscape, all she saw was darkness. Worse, her brother insisted on walking outside every few minutes to case the "grave"—that was the name they had given to the open pit left behind after digging up the truck. Opening and closing the side garage door allowed cold air to rush in. *Not good,* she thought. Plus, when Pete walked around outside, it made her nervous.

Later, after Derek arrived—he showed up at midnight, as promised—things settled down. The Brunellis broke out sandwiches and a flask of hot coffee. The threesome sat in the dark and told ghost stories. That usually made time fly by.

But not tonight, Kathy brooded. *This is just plain miserable.*

Finally, at 4:00 a.m., they called it quits. "We're hosed," Pete declared. "This guy's a no-show."

"Agreed," said Derek.

"Never again," Kathy groused on the way home. "Never."

"You big baby."

"Shut up."

PETE AND KATHY CHECKED IN WITH THE TWINS LATER THAT MORNING on a speakerphone call.

"It's close to noon, actually," Kathy corrected her brother.

"So what? It was a long night."

"I didn't hear you complaining."

"We camped out in the garage," Pete explained to the twins. "Your turn tonight. I left a space heater in there, and chairs we found. You'll have a good view of the place looking south—right toward the grave. Presuming the perp shows up with his flashlight again, you'll see him."

The twins lit up. "He's gotta be coming tonight," Tom said. "There's no chance he hasn't heard about the truck by now."

"We'll be ready," Suzanne said. "Heidi is joining in the fun too."

THE THREESOME WOULD BE ON THEIR OWN; DEREK HAD A STAKEOUT for another case on his schedule.

"But there'll be a deputy patrolling Highway 89," he assured the foursome during a speakerphone check-in, "all night. No matter what, she'll be ten minutes or less from you. Call me if the perp appears and I'll have the deputy race over."

The Jacksons and Heidi arrived together, just before midnight; Suzanne parked the Chevy in the Watsons' driveway. Jack's house was dark and quiet, the night inky black. The three hiked over to Hilda's place and moved straight into the garage. First up was turning on the space heater.

"Kathy was right," Suzanne whispered. "This place is freezing."

"You guys want to be police officers," Heidi taunted. "You'd better get used to this stuff. And we don't have to whisper. The creep can't hear us."

All three had dressed for the cold night with thick, warm socks, boots, jeans, and winter jackets. The twins had brought two pair of binoculars and, on the advice of the Brunellis, a thermos of hot coffee, plus food for three. It promised to be a long night.

"I figure the witching hours are between one and three a.m.," Suzanne said.

Heidi looked at her askance. "The 'witching hours?'"

"When evil is afoot!" Suzanne replied, laughing.

"That's when he'll show," Tom explained. "If he shows . . ."

Heidi wasn't holding her breath. "I hope you're right."

Time dragged. Every so often, one of the three picked up a pair of binoculars and scanned the view outside the garage's south-facing windows. Dim light projected from the outdoor security lights of the neighboring house to the east; to the west—Dave and Sarah's property —and straight back south was pure darkness. Still, a waning gibbous moon silvered the landscape. Seeing the grave from the garage proved next to impossible; however, they could lock onto its rough location.

At 1:00 a.m. Tom announced, "I'm going to sneak over to the grave and scout the area."

"What for?" Suzanne countered, scrunched down in her chair and clutching her knees. "It's freezing cold out there. And if he shows, we'll see him—or his silhouette at least—from here. Relax."

"The fresh air'll wake me up. Besides, you can watch my back."

Suzanne and Heidi focused on Tom, a moonlight-edged silhouette that trekked over to the pit, circled it once, and returned in less than three minutes.

"Man, it's cold out there," he reported.

"Told you."

Another hour slipped by before Tom's cell phone pinged: *Incoming message.* "What the heck," he said. "Who's messaging me at two-ten in the morning?" He tapped on the message. *"Dang,"* he whispered. "It's him! He's in the house!"

"Seriously?" Suzanne asked.

Heidi grabbed her camera and flipped it on.

"Seriously. Check him out." Tom held up his cell phone. The surveillance camera installed in the bookcase had captured a greyish still displaying a tallish man—wearing a handkerchief to hide his face—stepping through the front door and heading into the tiny living room. "How great is that? The guy just provided us with an early warning."

"No way could anyone identify him from that picture," Heidi snapped. She checked her camera settings.

Ping. Another incoming message. Tom knew that the messages lagged about thirty seconds behind the actual events. "He triggered it again." Tom touched the screen. "The guy walked out . . . What's he holding in his hand?"

"You're giving me goosebumps," Suzanne hissed.

"Next stop is the pit," Tom whispered.

Suzanne touched her cell phone and tapped on Derek's number. The detective answered on the first ring. "He's here."

Derek's voice sounded a million miles away. Or maybe it just felt that way. "The deputy is on her way."

"There he is!" Tom exclaimed. "He's halfway to the pit."

"I see him," Heidi said calmly. She didn't rattle easily. "He's moving fast too."

"I'll follow him," Tom said, heading for the side door. "Otherwise he'll pull a disappearing act again."

Suzanne wasn't buying it. "Listen, hotshot. It's dangerous out there. No heroics."

"No choice, watch my back." Tom ripped out the garage's side door and hustled toward the pit, ducking low and moving fast.

Heidi looped the camera strap around her neck and dropped her bag on the floor, rushing out behind Tom seconds later.

Suzanne followed them with her binoculars, tracking the three moonlit silhouettes south toward the pit, before the first shadow—the suspect's—vanished into thin air. *What? Where . . . ?*

Meanwhile, Tom slowed as he drew closer to the pit. *Where is he?* His heart beat like crazy. He reached the edge of the pit and peered down. A sound. Startled, he turned.

Suzanne whipped out of the garage. She had spotted Tom, standing over the pit, Heidi rushing up from behind, a shadow rising from the ground, one arm raised—something in its hand—striking, down, hard. Tom began to fall but turned, almost in slow motion. The arm rose again and—

Suzanne screamed. A sudden burst of blinding light lit the figure, frozen in time, then faded in an instant. The shadowy figure fled east, toward Highway 89.

Heidi reached the pit and dropped to the ground, peering into the darkness. "Tom. *Tom!*"

Nothing.

Suzanne fell to the earth beside her, lighting the depth with her camera's flashlight. Her brother lay at the bottom, all four limbs splayed out. "*Tom!* Are you okay?"

No answer.

Somewhere in the distance, a motorcycle fired up—a distinctive sound, but quieter than most motorbike engines, Suzanne thought.

The two clamored down the ragged dirt wall and knelt beside Tom, gently touching his face and shaking him. "Wake up!" Suzanne cried.

Heidi pinched Tom, hard.

He stirred and his eyelids flickered, looking up at them. "What—what happened?"

"He conked you, that's what happened!" Suzanne said. "Are you okay?"

"Define okay." Tom touched the crown of his head. "Ouch."

Heidi asked, "Can you stand?"

"I— Sure." He grabbed their hands and struggled to his feet, leaning against the dirt wall of the pit for support.

A flashlight clicked on above, startling the trio. "I'm Deputy Harper," a woman's voice called down. "Are you guys all right down there?"

"Yeah, we're fine," Suzanne replied. "The guy hit my brother on the head before he raced away."

"Did you get a look at him?"

"I didn't," Suzanne said. She closed her eyes and took a deep breath. *Calm down.*

"Well, I got a nice shot of him, with my flash," Heidi said, looking at the tiny screen on the back of her camera. "Unfortunately, the creep was wearing a handkerchief over his face. Did you see him, Tom?"

"Negative." He held his throbbing head with both hands now. "I never even heard him until the last second."

"One thing," Suzanne said, "after the guy ran off, I heard a motorcycle starting up."

"I heard it too," Heidi said.

"A motorcycle, huh," the deputy repeated. She straightened up. "Any idea which way it headed?"

Suzanne replayed the distinctive sound in her mind, the engine noise trailing away. "South, toward the city."

"Great. We'll arrange a nice little reception party."

19

A SILENT SUSPECT

Kathy received Suzanne's text message at 2:17 a.m. on Thursday, awakening her from a bad dream. . . something about spending an entire night in a freezing dark tunnel—by herself.

On the run, heading to Prescott. Perp is on a motorcycle. The sheriff is waiting for him.

Three minutes later, the Brunellis were in the Mustang with Pete at the wheel, traveling north on 89. Soon, in the distance, just as they crossed outside the city limits, they spotted flashing blue and red lights.

"Deputies," Kathy said.

"Gotta be."

As they grew closer, they saw two patrol cars blocking the southbound lane heading into the city. Traffic was sparse, but a semi had slowed before deputies waved the driver on.

"Hey, there's Derek," Pete said. He pulled the Mustang over to the right side of the road, his wheels touching grass, and came to a stop. The detective turned and waved to them before he came over.

"Hi, how 'ya doing? I'm guessing you heard from the twins.

We're looking for that motorcycle." A Ford SUV slowed, and the deputies waved him through.

"We haven't talked to them," Kathy replied. She had called three times, but there was no answer. "What happened?"

"The perp showed. First, he walked into the house and your camera messaged Tom. Then Tom shadowed him out to the pit. He got a knock on his head for the effort. The suspect escaped on a motorcycle."

"Tom hit the guy?"

"Nope. The guy hammered Tom."

"Is Tom all right?" Kathy asked quietly.

"Yeah, I believe so. Wait a sec— Is that what I think it is?"

A motorcycle appeared around the curve to the north, heading toward them. It slowed as it approached the roadblock.

Derek hustled back to the deputies. The three officers waited as the motorcycle came to a stop. As the Brunellis watched in rapt attention, the driver shut off his engine and stepped away from the bike. Tall and thin, he didn't move like a young person, but the siblings couldn't see his face in the dark—no way to confirm his age.

A conversation ensued. Just a couple of minutes later, the deputies handcuffed the man, walked him over to a police cruiser, and guided him into the backseat.

Derek waved the Brunellis over. "Do you recognize this guy?"

The siblings scrutinized the man through the side window. "Nope," Pete said.

"Me neither. Did you get his name?" Kathy asked the detective.

"He refused to give it. Says he wants to talk to his lawyer. I'm running his license plate now. He's carrying a big old .45 revolver, and there's fresh blood on the butt of the gun. I'm guessing that might be Tom's blood."

"He used a *gun* on Tom?" Kathy asked.

"He's okay."

"Can he refuse to identify himself?" Pete asked.

"Sure, but his license plate's a giveaway, unless the bike is stolen. Headquarters is running it now."

Another patrol car appeared around the curve, lights flashing, heading toward the now-open roadblock. It was leading a white Chevy: the Jacksons'.

The two vehicles pulled in behind the parked motorcycle. The twins and Heidi jumped out of the car and hurried over to Detective Robinson and the Brunellis.

"You got him?" Suzanne shouted.

"If it's the same guy, yes," Derek replied.

Kathy looked closely at Tom. "Were you hurt?"

"Nah, I'm just a little woozy." He stroked the back of his head.

Pete couldn't help himself. "We heard you donated a little blood."

Derek pointed the suspect out in the back of the patrol car. "See if you recognize him."

Tom and Suzanne crossed over to the vehicle and peered in. Heidi stood right behind them.

"Dr. Ritter!" the twins chorused.

The man turned, his ashen face a blank page punctuated with dull eyes.

Click. Flash. Heidi had her shot.

"Dr. Ritter?" Pete asked. "Who the heck is he?"

"The vet, right?" Kathy quizzed. "The one you took Rex to see?"

"That's him, all right," Suzanne replied. "Dr. Richard Ritter. I can hardly believe it."

"That's odd," Pete said, "So the initials Hilda penned don't make sense."

"Well, he's gotta be the mystery guy in the photo," Kathy said. "Right?"

"I can't—Ritter tried to poison Hilda," Suzanne said, trying to wrap her mind around it.

"Carfentanil," said Tom.

"Of course," Pete said. "He's a vet, with a country practice that includes large animals. I'll bet he stocks the stuff."

"At the very least," Kathy said, "he has access to the drug. We should've thought of that."

Detective Robinson opened the back door of the patrol vehicle.

"The motorcycle is registered to a Dr. Richard Ritter. Would that be you, sir?"

"I'm not saying a word," the man responded, "until I talk to my attorney."

"Well, that's your right," Derek said, shutting the door again. He turned to the others. "We'll run him down to the Sheriff's Office and book him."

"If he's the getaway guy," Tom said, "it's way past the statute of limitations."

"Sure, the hijacking, the theft," Derek said. "But if he's the one who tried to poison Hilda Wyndham, he'll be facing serious charges. Plus someone's blood is on the butt of that gun, and I'm betting it's yours. That's assault with a deadly weapon—even if he didn't use it to shoot at you. A serious felony. No matter what, he's earned himself a cozy little spot at Arizona State Prison." Almost as an afterthought, he added, "I hope he enjoys it there."

More police cars pulled up in the night. Sheriff McClennan arrived with the Chief right behind him.

"It's beginning to look like a police convention," Kathy quipped.

The Chief rushed over to Tom. "What happened?"

"Nothing major, Dad. He just conked me a good one, that's all."

"With what?"

"An old .45," Derek replied. "Haven't seen one like it in years."

The Chief groaned.

"After he got hit, Tom fell into the pit," Suzanne explained.

"Suzie, I'm fine," Tom said. "You're being overly dramatic."

"You're lucky you didn't break an arm—or worse," the Chief said, seething. He stared over at the suspect. "Your mother won't like this. Is that him?"

Detective Robinson filled the two senior officers in on the arrest as the mystery searchers and Heidi listened. "The guy drove right up to our roadblock, as if there wasn't a thing wrong. Said he couldn't sleep and took the bike for a spin, but he was carrying a .45 revolver with fresh blood on the butt. He couldn't explain how the blood got there. His name is Dr. Richard Ritter—"

"You gotta be kidding me," the sheriff exclaimed, his eyebrows arching up. "Dick Ritter's my vet—he looks after my dogs! What's he got to do with a forty-five year old hijacking?"

"Dick Ritter!" Suzanne uttered.

"Sure," the sheriff replied. "His friends call him that. It's short for Richard."

Tom groaned. "Of course. 'D.R.'—Dick Ritter, not Dave Ratzinger. Boy, were we ever wrong."

Meanwhile, Heidi continued working unobtrusively, even slipping back to the patrol car to grab another quick photo of the suspect through the window. He turned away.

"That works," she told the mystery searchers, showing off the image on her camera's screen. "Even trying to hide his face, Dick will look just fine on the front page."

2 0

A DEAL

The mystery searchers slept until noon. An incoming message from Derek awakened Suzanne: *Meeting at the Sheriff's Office ASAP.*

Suzanne replied: *On our way.*

"Oh, boy," Tom said when she had shaken him awake. "This should be interesting."

Suzanne called to alert the Brunellis. "We'll pick you up. Have you guys eaten?"

"I have," Kathy replied. "But Pete's still stuffing his face."

On their way downtown, the four discussed the dramatic events of the previous night and the upcoming meeting.

"Ritter never crossed anyone's mind," Suzanne claimed. "I mean, why would he?"

"Carfentanil—that should have tipped us off," Kathy argued. "It would only make sense that a vet would handle that stuff. We just presumed that the drug had to come from street trafficking."

"What the heck," Pete countered. "That stuff is for elephants. There's a shortage of them around here."

"I'll bet he used it on horses," Tom said.

"What's this meeting about?" Kathy asked.

"Your guess is as good as mine," Suzanne replied.

Pete said, "You can count on Ritter being lawyered up by now."

Suzanne asked, "What do you think, Tom?"

"I think Ritter talked."

Suzanne located a parking spot close to the downtown Sheriff's Offices. Soon, the mystery searchers trailed one another into a large conference room. Derek sat across from Heidi as she scribbled in her large notebook.

"Good afternoon," the detective said, standing up to greet the foursome. "Everybody get some sleep?"

"Did we ever," Kathy said. "How about you guys?"

"I did, but the constabulary never rests," Heidi joked.

"That's the truth," Derek replied with a woeful grin. "But I managed to squeeze in a few hours. Please sit down." He glanced up and slid his chair along the table. "Hang on. Here come the sheriffs."

Sheriff McClennan and Coconino County Sheriff Rich Connor entered the conference room.

"Hello, hello," Sheriff McClennan greeted everyone. "Good to see y'all are looking rested. You remember Sheriff Connor, right?"

Everyone stood and shook hands. The air was electric with anticipation.

"The Chief is joining us in—oh, wait, here he is now. We need another chair. Come on in, Ed."

The meeting kicked off with Sheriff McClennan leading. A printed document rested on the desk in front of him. "Well, the reason I've asked everyone here today is to advise you that Dr. Ritter has agreed to cooperate under certain conditions." He glanced over at the twins. "The district attorney was very astute. Your father and I—together with Sheriff Connor and Detective Robinson—all agree with him. And we want to share the details with you."

He paused to gather his thoughts. "As we all know, the statute of limitations prevents the state from charging Ritter for the hijacking of the armored truck. However, thanks to you, Tom, we had another card to play. In Arizona, the penalty for assault with a deadly weapon is five to fifteen years in prison and up to a hundred-and-fifty-thousand dollar fine. When Ritter hammered you with his revolver, he probably didn't have a clue what he set himself up for. But he soon found out."

"Ritter folded fast," Derek said, "as soon as we told him we'd recovered traces of carfentanil from Hilda's mug and that we knew he used it in his vet practice. The district attorney offered to omit the fine and reduce the charges down if he confessed. The state will be charging Ritter with both the assault and felony manslaughter, plus a slew of other related counts. The state gets to skip a trial and go directly to sentencing. I'll skip the technicalities."

"So the good news is that Hilda Wyndham's cry for justice has been answered," Heidi said.

Sheriff McClennan turned to her. "It sure has, Heidi, and your contribution—and that of *The Daily Pilot*—is deeply appreciated."

She shot him a thumbs up.

"We have Ritter's confession already, but he has agreed to provide us with the entire background story of the heist and the getaway," Sheriff Connor added. "All of it."

"Not that it will matter much," the Chief added. "It'll be a long time before he ever sees daylight again."

Heidi was scribbling as fast as she could. It would make a heck of a story.

Suzanne giggled. "So, Tom, it turns out that your conk on the head was a real blessing."

"Want to hear something weird?" Derek asked. "The handgun he hit you with is the same .45 they used in the hijacking! It belonged to Ritter's father."

"Hasn't seen action for forty-five years," Kathy joked.

"Oh, man, that's a strange coincidence." Tom touched the bump for the umpteenth time. "How long will he serve behind bars?"

"Depends on the judge," Sheriff McClennan replied. "But you can count on a long haul."

"Bye-bye, Dick," Pete quipped.

The sheriff leafed through the document. "Derek is going to

handle the interview with Ritter. We'll tape it, but we thought it would be nice for one of you to sit in. Without the four of you, we'd never have sorted this case out."

"Ritter's attorney agreed to it," the Chief said. He glanced at his watch. "We'll start in a few minutes. But his lawyer insisted on one stipulation: Tom can't attend the meeting."

"Why not?" Tom asked, his head tilting back.

"Because you're the guy he thumped."

"Count me out," Suzanne said, glowering. "I don't want to be in the same room as that. . . that creep."

"I volunteer!" Pete crowed.

His sister eyed him. "Flip for it."

The Chief laughed. He reached into his pocket and pulled out a quarter. "Call it!"

"Heads," Pete said.

"It's tails."

Sheriff McClellan stood up. "Okay. Let's go say hello."

21

REVELATIONS

E arly Friday morning, Sheriff McClennan called the twins. "The people on Sidewinder Lane are worrying about the recent events at Hilda Wyndham's," he said. "Let's set up a neighborhood meeting for this afternoon at four thirty. We need to allay their fears."

After lunch, the foursome dragged some folding chairs out of storage and drove out to Hilda's place. They spaced them apart in her living room with a little help from Heidi.

The girls had made a point of calling Bill and Rita Halliday to invite them to attend. Then the mystery searchers and Heidi canvassed the entire neighborhood door to door. The Watsons and Lynn Whitewood agreed to come. So did seven other neighbors. Even grumpy Burt Moore expressed interest.

Dave Ratzinger was happy to see them. The friendly rancher and his wife were humbled by the recent news about Hilda's will. "We had no idea," Dave said.

D<small>ETECTIVE</small> R<small>OBINSON AND THE TWO SHERIFFS ARRIVED JUST AFTER</small>
four o'clock.

"They're the star attraction," Suzanne commented with a wry
grin. "Without them, no one would bother showing up."

"Except Jack," Kathy quipped. "And here he comes."

Sure enough, Jack and his father were at the front door with
Dave and Sarah—and Rex, of course, pushed in between them.

"Come right on in," Kathy said.

The dog barked at the two officers before he whipped into the
kitchen, dodging chairs as the mystery searchers gave Jack a high-
five.

"Good thing you set your alarm when all this began," Kathy
joked.

"That's a fact," Suzanne agreed. "Otherwise, we wouldn't have
had a clue that Dr. Ritter was skulking around here in the middle of
the night."

The officers congratulated Jack too; Heidi took the boy's picture
as he shook hands with the two sheriffs. "You'll be famous
tomorrow morning," she teased. "Look for yourself on the front
page of the newspaper."

"Rex too?" the boy asked.

"You bet."

Jack beamed, and so did his father. Dave and Sarah gave Jack a
big hug, much to his embarrassment, telling the boy he was almost
like an adopted son to them.

The Hallidays came early too. "We haven't been inside this house
for forty-some years," Bill said. "The house looks so much smaller
than I remember it."

"It's sad," Rita declared. "Robert and his mother were special
people."

Soon, the tiny living room filled up. Folding chairs stretched
into the kitchen and down the hall. Kathy turned the heat off; with
everyone crowded in, it had grown uncomfortably warm.

"We're ready," Tom announced. The murmur of voices died

down. "If anyone else shows up, they'll have to stand." Polite chuckles circled the living room.

Sheriff McClennan stood up to address the crowd. "As you're aware, Mrs. Hilda Wyndham passed earlier in December. The medical examiner labeled it a 'suspicious death.' The crime lab found traces of a dangerous drug in Hilda's coffee mug, but it turned out the lady died from a cardiac arrest. We figured someone tried to poison her, but she passed away from fright. Then, as many of you witnessed a couple days ago, Prescott's own mystery searchers led us to unearth an armored truck buried on federal government land, right behind Hilda's property. The suspect in both cases—and they're connected—is now behind bars."

An explosion of voices burst out.

The sheriff raised both hands until the noise died down. "This individual has offered his full cooperation. In doing so, he revealed what happened out here—in the last few days and long ago too. I'm now going to turn the meeting over to Kathy Brunelli and her fellow mystery searchers."

"Wait a minute, Sheriff!" Dave called out. "Who did you arrest? Is it anyone we know?"

"I'm sure you'll recognize his name: Dr. Richard Ritter."

Another outburst of voices rang out, this time tinged with anger.

Burt Moore led the charge: "You're putting us on. You've arrested Dick Ritter, our veterinarian?"

"Yes, we have," Sheriff McClennan said.

"That's just plain crazy."

"It is, sir, I know. Fortunately, the man has admitted his guilt."

After that, Burt Moore fell silent for a while.

Over the next hour, the mystery searchers—aided now and then by the three police officers—detailed the entire story.

"Go ahead, Kathy," the sheriff said. "Run with it."

"Okay." She stood, nervous at first—public speaking wasn't her favorite thing. "I—I'll begin with Robert Wyndham and Dr. Ritter meeting at the YMCA during Robert's senior year in high school.

Dick, a year older, had already graduated in Phoenix, before his family had moved to Prescott. The two boys soon realized they had something in common: they both loved true crime stories. Somehow, in their many discussions, they imagined one of their own: the hijacking of an armored truck with lots of money in it."

Sheriff Connor jumped in to explain the details of the heist itself. One of the older couples said that they vaguely remembered the strange disappearance of an armored truck.

"The idea," Kathy continued, "was to commit the perfect crime by making the truck—and the money—disappear forever. And it kinda worked—until now. Years earlier, as you all know, the Krause family had deeded most of Sidewinder Ranch to the federal government. The boys buried the truck on federal government land—"

"Because no one ever went out there, and the land would remain untouched forever," Pete interrupted.

"There was a big hitch in their plans," Kathy said. "To avoid the Highway Patrol after the robbery, they took the back roads from Williams to Jerome—in the armored truck. No way was that a picnic. If you slip off that narrow road, it's a *long* way to the bottom. It's a miracle they made it."

"Ritter admitted to us that it panicked them," Derek said, "and that it took them much longer to navigate the dangerous gravel road than they expected. There were some scary moments."

"But they finally reached Sidewinder Lane at four in the morning, driving slowly, with all the truck's lights off," Kathy continued. "From 89 they turned onto the service road behind the properties, followed by another turn to coast right into the pit. Or the 'grave,' as we call it."

"But first," Suzanne explained, "Ritter jumped out and Robert cut the engine; he coasted into the grave on the partial ramp. Then he crawled out the back doors. They shoveled as much of the dirt as they could on top of the truck with shovels, finishing just before sunrise."

"Where did the money go?" Hal asked.

"Into their backpacks," Tom spoke up, "and buried in the barn until the hue and cry died down. Later the next day, Robert did a little more 'landscaping' with Ritter's help. They covered the armored truck so that it wouldn't see light again until—"

"Rex pointed the way," Heidi reasoned aloud.

22

THE DEED

Late-afternoon gloom had silently seeped into Hilda's house, darkening the mood of the crowd. Suzanne stood and turned on lights in the living room, kitchen and hallway.

Lynn Whitewood raised an arm. "I have a question. How on earth did they dig a hole that big?"

Tom explained. "Well, Robert's father, Troy Wyndham—he died long before all this took place—had bought a mechanical digger years earlier from a bankruptcy auction. He wanted to deepen and broaden the natural pond at the rear of the property. The digger's still out back, behind the barn, sunk into the ground."

"Robert had dug the pit the previous evening," Suzanne said. "He told his Mom he wanted to build up the berm surrounding the pond, and that required loads of dirt. The boys slipped onto the federal land at dusk and dug the pit with an earth ramp sloping down into it."

A burly man stood up in the hallway. "Wouldn't a neighbor wonder why they dug it?"

"The boys had their story, but no one asked," Derek said, "Remember, these homes are quite apart from one another. It's a few acres between houses."

"Did Mrs. Wyndham have any involvement in the crime?" Rita Halliday asked in a timid voice.

"She did not," Derek replied.

"I'm glad."

"In fact," Suzanne said, "Hilda didn't find out the truth until several years later. She had a hard time making property payments, so Robert paid off the mortgage. She wondered where the money came from—running a bookstore doesn't pay that well. He finally fessed up."

"Hilda regretted having accepted the money from that day onward," Kathy said. "Thus, the Bible verse that Hilda had copied down, which we found when we were looking for clues here in the house."

Suzanne read the words aloud: "'Cast away all the crimes you have committed, and make for yourselves a new heart and a new spirit! Why should you die. . .?'"

HEADS NODDED IN SOLEMN SILENCE AROUND THE ROOM UNTIL BILL Halliday spoke up for the first time. "But Hilda didn't commit a crime."

"No, but she lived in a house bought with the proceeds," Pete said.

"The guilt ate her up," Tom said.

"That's right," Kathy said, nodding. "Robert Wyndham and Dick Ritter split one hundred and twenty-five thousand dollars between them. They agreed not to spend any of the cash for at least a year, to avoid attracting attention. That was a major component of their 'perfect crime.' Dick's share put him through veterinary school and allowed him to open his practice. Robert bought a new car, then later another. And a few years later, he paid off his mother's mortgage."

"But the crime divided the boys," she added. "Their mutual trust eroded. Each was afraid the other would somehow reveal the heist.

They stopped being friends. Dr. Ritter claimed they seldom ever talked again. Years passed."

The mystery searchers reached the part where Dr. Ritter drove out to Hilda's place for the fateful meeting with her.

"Christmastime must have made her feel aware of her solitude, her loneliness," Suzanne said. "We think the holidays reminded her of the premature deaths of her husband and her son." She passed the prayer card out, where it traveled from hand to hand, and told the crowd how Pete found it near the pond. "Hilda reached out to Dr. Ritter the day before Christmas Eve, informing him she intended to call the authorities and reveal the truck's location. She promised not to expose Ritter's role in the hijacking and getaway—to say that her son had never identified his accomplice."

"But Ritter didn't believe her," Tom said. "He was sure that the Sheriff's Office would get the truth out of her. So he arranged a meeting the next morning at six a.m."

"Christmas Eve," Kathy reminded their rapt audience. "Just to 'talk it over,' as he told her. But he had already decided—"

"That if he could change her mind, fine. If not . . ." Pete, ever the most dramatic one of the four, traced a finger across his throat.

"He showed up in his veterinarian scrubs," Kathy said. "A dark blue outfit. . . because his next appointment was on a cattle ranch further north at 8 a.m."

"Which finally explained 'why' Rex barked at everyone with a uniform on," Suzanne said. "Ritter had freaked the dog out."

"No way could he change Hilda's mind," Kathy continued. "While she was reaching into the fridge for cream, he poured poison into her coffee mug: carfentanil, a powerful opiate that vets sometimes use. But before she even sat down at the kitchen table, Mrs. Wyndham suffered a cardiac arrest and collapsed on the kitchen floor. Right in front of a shocked Ritter."

The neighbors looked at one another in astonishment.

"Oh, Lord!" Barb Ratzinger exclaimed. "Poor Hilda." Her husband squeezed her hand.

Hal Watson spoke for the first time. "Why didn't he just call nine-one-one? Dead people don't talk."

"The medical examiner believes Hilda was still alive for up to an hour after the heart attack," Derek said.

There was a collective gasp.

Bill Halliday sat bolt upright, shocked. "You mean he walked out, just like that, leaving her alone?"

"Yes," Kathy said. "Right after he had threatened her life. He refused to tell us his exact words, but whatever he said frightened her so much that she collapsed to the floor in front of the refrigerator. Ritter thought she'd fainted, but after checking her vital signs, he realized Hilda had experienced a serious cardiac event. Then he abandoned her."

The crowd fell deathly quiet.

Jack raised his hand. "That night when Dr. Ritter returned, why did he come into the house?"

"The coffee mugs," Tom replied. "He read the story in *The Daily Pilot*, of course... about finding a dangerous drug in her kitchen. He had to see if the mugs were still there. They weren't."

"Wait—Ritter broke in here?" Dave asked.

"He didn't have to," Tom replied. "He stole an extra set of keys off a hook in the kitchen before he left on Christmas Eve."

"I have a key too," Dave said. "She asked me to keep one in case she ever had a medical problem. You know, she felt quite alone and vulnerable."

"But *we* found another set of keys that Ritter came back for," Pete said. "The keys to the armored car—at the bottom of the pond."

"Ritter admitted that he'd become kind of paranoid after the *Pilot* published the photo Hilda snapped forty-five years earlier," Kathy said. "His mistake was going into the pond to look for the keys. That's what tipped us off."

"And the reason we went searching for a buried truck," finished Pete.

A young homeowner in the hallway stood up. "What about the

statute of limitations? After forty-some years, the police couldn't charge Ritter with armed robbery, right?"

"Right," the sheriff replied. "By law, we have to lay charges within *seven* years or we're out of luck. Ritter knew that and couldn't have cared less. What worried him was his standing in the community. If his role in the hijacking ever got out, his veterinary clientele would evaporate."

He locked eyes with Burt Moore. "Like you, for instance, sir. Would you have continued to seek Dr. Ritter's services for your pets?"

"Not a chance."

"That's what I figured."

"What about Rex?" Jack asked, looking down to the dog asleep at his feet. "How did he end up at Watson Lake?" He leaned over to pet his best friend.

"After Hilda collapsed, the dog began barking like crazy," Derek replied. "Mr. Moore told me he heard the noise across the lane. Ritter panicked—he worried that someone would come looking. So he grabbed Rex and slipped a couple grains of carfentanil into his mouth. The poor mutt fell unconscious within seconds."

"Then," Tom said, "he threw Rex into his car—one he had borrowed from an employee at the clinic—and dropped him off at Watson Lake on the way back to town."

"There wasn't a soul out there," Suzanne said. "When Rex regained consciousness—whenever that was—all he would have known is that something bad had happened to Hilda and that he had landed in a strange environment."

"And he was on his own," Kathy said, her voice catching. "Lost. A stray."

"Lucky for Rex, *you* found him," Jack said.

"*He* found *them*," Heidi reminded everyone.

Dave leaned down and scratched the dog's neck. "Rex is special, for sure. Every time we walked on this property, he'd end up lying right over that buried truck."

Sheriff McClennan guffawed. "Rex was trying to show us Hilda's secret, but we weren't listening."

The front door opened. The Chief squeezed into the crowded, tiny living room and apologized for arriving late. He removed his gold-braided hat. "Sorry. Another case held me up."

Rex growled, jumped up, and barked twice at the uniformed officer. The mystery searchers broke into infectious laughter. People clapped and joined in the fun.

The Chief grinned. "What'd I say?" he asked.

Suzanne doubled over. "Oh, Dad." She could hardly get the words out. "You're cracking us up, you really are!"

EXCERPT FROM BOOK 8

The Hunt for the Elusive Mastermind

Chapter 1:
The Set-up

Summer vacation had finally—*at last*—arrived in Prescott. It was a perfect warm day in June with bright, Arizona-blue skies for as far as anyone could see. A gentle cooling breeze wafted in from the northern heights, fresh, forest-clean air. Sounds of summer floated through the city's neighborhoods: birds sang, lawnmowers droned, and children shrieked with laughter. Somewhere in the distance a dog barked, and a baby cried.

For the Jackson twins—Tom and Suzanne—it was idyllic. The first day of their summer break from Prescott High was always the most promising, delicious day of the year. At least, that was *their* plan . . .

The twins headed out to Whiskey Row, Prescott's historic downtown district, a throwback to the Old West days that had evolved into a tourist and shopping destination. They intended to drop by Hall's Hardware, a corner store on Cortez Street, at the "request" of their father, Chief Edward Jackson of the Prescott City Police. He had surprised them at breakfast that morning. . . or "Entrapped us!" as Tom laughingly quipped to Suzanne on their way out of the house.

"Any plans for today?" the Chief had asked, sounding quite innocent as he sipped his second cup of coffee.

"Nothing big," Suzanne replied. "I might go shopping with Kathy."

"Not working at the St. Vincent de Paul Donation Center?"

"Nope, not this week. Mrs. Otto doesn't have enough used books to price."

"What about you, Tom?"

Tom glanced over toward his father with a raised eyebrow. "Pete and I talked about tennis, that's about it."

"Great!" their father replied, beaming. "Because the picket fence needs painting, front and back."

The twins shot each other a look of despair. "Gee, Dad," Suzanne protested, "we just painted it a few years ago. It's the first day of summer vacation. Can't it wait?"

"Time out," Tom hastened to add. "That fence is in great shape— it doesn't look bad at all. Just ask Mom. In fact, it looks fantastic!" If there was one thing Tom disliked, painting fences was at the top of the list.

"Uh-huh. Please pick up four gallons of white paint at Hall's Hardware this morning. Charge it to my account." He grinned. "Enough for two coats. Shouldn't take you more than a couple days. Get a gallon of primer too, in case scraping off that loose paint takes you down to bare wood."

One thing about the Chief: few people argued with him. Except for the twins' mother, of course. Sherri argued—especially when she thought her children's safety was at stake. And she won, too. Sometimes.

An hour later, as they drove downtown in their Chevy Impala, the twins kicked around the morning's curveball.

"Speaking for myself, I never even saw it coming," Suzanne moaned.

Her brother laughed. "Dad had it all figured out. See, it's the element of surprise, essential in fighting crime—and household maintenance. Did you message the Brunellis?"

"Uh-huh. I explained that management had conscripted us into forced labor. Maybe they'll be willing to help."

Kathy and Pete Brunelli were the twins' best friends. The four had grown close in elementary school; later, when they graduated to Prescott High, the foursome had teamed up to solve mysteries. Their successes in that endeavor had planted them on the front page of the city's hometown newspaper, *The Daily Pilot.* Along the way, the paper's star reporter—Heidi Hoover—had emerged as one of their biggest fans, dubbing them "the mystery searchers." The name stuck.

Suzanne drove as the twins headed downtown toward Court- house Square, the cultural heart of Prescott. The quiet central Arizona city of fifty thousand was renowned for its four-seasons climate: high desert, rolling hills with mountains in the distance, close to the immense Prescott National Forest. Her route took them past police headquarters. As she turned onto Gurley Street, four unmarked police cars—one after another, no lights or sirens— whipped out of the police parking lot, cranked hard right, and sped away.

Tom sat bolt upright. "Hey, we've never seen that before. What the heck—"

"Here come two more." Sure enough, two unmarked police sedans pulled out, heading in the same direction as the first four— and just as fast too.

"Did you see who was driving the last vehicle?"

"Uh-huh, Detective Joe Ryan," Suzanne replied. They had known the low-key investigator since childhood. The Chief often referred to him as "the best man on the force," and he enjoyed a well- deserved reputation for solving crimes. The mystery searchers had worked with him on a number of previous cases.

"*Wait!*" Tom exclaimed. "Pull over, Suzie." His sister had already passed the police station.

"What for?"

"Something big is happening. Let's go say hello to Dad."

At that moment, a huge old Caddy backed out of a parking spot on busy Courthouse Square. Suzanne nosed the Chevy in and the twins jumped out of the car. Tom plugged the parking meter before they hiked back two blocks, all uphill on the slanting sidewalks. They pushed open the front door of police headquarters, just in time to see their father rushing out of his office.

Instead of his immaculate blue uniform, he had changed into jeans and a short-sleeve shirt. *Very unusual,* Suzanne noted.

"Dad!" Tom shouted, his voice ricocheting off the marble walls. His father stopped in his tracks and swiveled toward them.

"Hey, what are you two doing here?"

"We spotted all the police cars rushing off," Tom explained.

"We're just nosy," Suzanne admitted, a little sheepishly.

The Chief smiled. "Since you're here . . . C'mon, I think you'll find this interesting."

Years earlier, the twins had decided to follow their father's footsteps into law enforcement, a development that he encouraged at every opportunity.

The three Jacksons jumped into an unmarked cruiser. Relentless two-way radio chatter clamored on low volume—something about a stakeout.

"Our destination is only two blocks away," the Chief said as he pulled onto Gurley Street. "We don't want to draw attention to ourselves."

Suzanne sat in the front seat, staring intently ahead. "What's happening, Dad?"

"You remember Ben Walters, the president of Prescott's Metro Bank?"

"Oh, sure," Tom said. "He's the guy who sponsors the Prescott Art Festival every year. He goes to our church."

"Uh-huh. Someone kidnapped his wife this morning, right after he left for work."

Suzanne gasped. "Kidnapped Mrs. Walters? From their *home?*"

"Affirmative. And we don't have a clue where she is. Walters received a phone call first thing when he arrived at his office. Whoever the kidnappers are, they demanded all the money in the bank's safe for her release—or else." The Chief pulled into a parking spot on Courthouse Square, just three spaces from the twins' white

Chevrolet. "And we're talking about a considerable amount of cash . . . far more than normal, in fact."

The Chief paused before opening the car door. "Just walk easy, like we're shopping—the kidnappers could be watching. Follow my lead." He grabbed a handheld two-way radio and stuffed it into his pants pocket.

Now the twins understood why their father had changed out of his uniform.

All three stepped out into the street. The Chief stopped to feed the parking meter before the trio sauntered along the sidewalk. At the red light on Cortez and Gurley Streets, they waited with a group of talkative, excited shoppers until the green light flashed WALK.

Diagonally across from the Yavapai Courthouse stood a building built in 1901, one of the city's national landmarks: the old Prescott National Bank, now converted into a large retail store at ground level. The twins knew it well. Just north of the intersection, on the east side of Cortez Street, appeared a service entrance—right beside a loading zone—that led straight into the center of the structure. The entrance was so narrow that most people walked past it without ever noticing.

"Here we are," the Chief said without glancing back. He ducked into the slender opening, the twins trailing close behind.

Dated-looking concrete-and-steel stairs climbed up to a second story, or down to the basement level. The Chief led the way up and used a key to open the second-floor security door. Then they turned right, heading down a dimly lit corridor with multiple doors. *Apartments,* Tom figured.

At the end of the corridor, the Chief unlocked a door and pushed it open.

"It's somebody's home," Suzanne blurted as they stepped into a tiny living room. A sweet, perfume-y aroma permeated the air. "Oh, what a beautiful cat."

A large orange tabby—rudely awakened from a sleeping position on the sofa—took one look at the three strangers and tore off down a hallway.

"Pretty, but shy," said Tom.

"This apartment belongs to Officer Williams's girlfriend, Stephanie Burke. She gave us permission to use it and dropped the keys off at the station just minutes ago. Don't turn on the lights." The Chief crossed into a small kitchen with a rear-facing window and slowly adjusted the horizontal blinds so they angled downward, offering a discreet view of the alleyway below. "Okay." He took a deep breath. "Whatever you do, don't move the blinds. Look down. What do you see?"

The twins squeezed in and stared hard. "A huge industrial dumpster," Tom said, "just a couple feet from the building."

The Chief nodded as he glanced at his watch. "Mr. Walters is going to deposit eight bags full of large currency bills in that dumpster in twenty minutes—at ten-thirty a.m. sharp."

"Those were the kidnappers' instructions?" Tom asked.

"Correct."

"After that," Suzanne said, "the kidnappers grab the money and run, right?"

"That's their plan. They told Walters they'd release his wife, unharmed, *after* they make their getaway—with the cash."

"So they threatened to harm her," Tom said, "if things went bad, right?"

"In no uncertain terms," the Chief said ominously.

"No clue where they would leave her?" Suzanne asked.

"Nope."

"You don't dare arrest them, but you can tail them," Tom reasoned aloud. "They have to know that."

"You'd sure think so."

Doubt began seeping into Suzanne's mind. "Wait a sec . . . Isn't it suspicious that the kidnappers set up a money transfer here, in the middle of downtown. . . in broad daylight? I mean—they gotta know they're being watched, right? That's obvious . . ."

The Chief looked at his daughter, trying hard to suppress a smile. "Yes. Strange, isn't it?"

To be continued. . .

I hope you have enjoyed this sneak peak at book 8 in
The Mystery Searchers Family Book Series

The Hunt for the Elusive Mastermind

To be released Spring, 2021

BIOGRAPHY

Barry Forbes began his writing career in 1980, eventually scripting and producing hundreds of film and video corporate presentations, winning a handful of industry awards along the way. At the same time, he served as an editorial writer for Tribune Newspapers and wrote his first two books, both non-fiction.

In 1997, he founded and served as CEO for Sales Simplicity Software, a market leader which was sold two decades later.

What next? "I always loved mystery stories and one of my favorite places to visit was Prescott, Arizona. It's situated in rugged central Arizona with tremendous locales for mysteries." In 2017, Barry merged his interest in mystery and his skills in writing, adding in a large dollop of technology. The Mystery Searchers Family Book Series was born.

Barry's wife, Linda, passed in 2019 and the series is dedicated to her. "Linda proofed the initial drafts of each book and acted as my chief advisor." The couple had been married for 49 years and had two children. A number of their fifteen grandchildren provided feedback on each book.

Contact Barry: barry@mysterysearchers.com

Book 1: The Mystery on Apache Canyon Drive

A small child wanders across a busy Arizona highway! In a hair-raising rescue, sixteen-year old twins Tom and Suzanne Jackson save the little girl from almost certain death. Soon, the brother and sister team up with best friends Kathy and Pete Brunelli on a perilous search for the child's past. The mystery deepens as one becomes two, forcing the deployment of secretive technology tools along Apache Canyon Drive. The danger level ramps up with the action, and the "mystery searchers" are born.

Book 2: The Ghost in the County Courthouse

A mysterious "ghost" bypasses the security system of Yavapai Courthouse Museum and makes off with four of the museum's most precious Native American relics. The mystery searchers, at the invitation of curator Dr. William Wasson, jump into the case and deploy a range of technology tools to discover the ghost's secrets. If the ghost strikes again, the museum's very future is in doubt. A dangerous game of cat and mouse ensues.

Book 3: The Secrets of the Mysterious Mansion

Heidi Hoover, a good friend and newspaper reporter for *The Daily Pilot*, introduces the mystery searchers to a mysterious mansion in the forest—at midnight! The mansion is under siege from unknown "hunters." *Who are they? What are they searching for?* Good, old-fashioned detective work and a couple of technology tools ultimately reveal the truth. A desperate race ensues, but time is running out.

Book 4: The House on Cemetery Hill

There's a dead man walking and it's up to the mystery searchers to figure out "why." That's the challenge from Mrs. Leslie McPherson, a successful but eccentric Prescott businesswoman. The mystery searchers team up with their favorite detective and utilize technology to spy on high-tech criminals at Cemetery Hill. It's a perilous game with heart-stopping moments.

Book 5: The Treasure of Skull Valley

Suzanne discovers a map hidden in the pages of a classic old book at the thrift store. It's titled "My Treasure Map" and leads past Skull Valley, twenty miles west of Prescott and into the high desert country—to an unexpected, shocking and elusive treasure. "Please help," the note begs. The mystery searchers utilize the power and reach of the Internet to trace the movement of people and events. . . half a century earlier.

Book 6: The Vanishing in Deception Gap

A text message to Kathy sets off a race into the unknown. "There are pirates operating out here and they're dangerous. I can't prove it, but I need your help." Who sent the message? Out where? Pirates! How weird is that? The mystery searchers dive in, but it might be too late. *The man has vanished into thin air.*

Book 7: The Getaway Lost in Time

A stray dog saves the twins from a dangerous predator on the hiking trail at Watson Lake. In a surprising twist, the dog leads the mystery searchers to the suspicious death of Hilda Wyndham, and a crime lost in time. They join the Sheriff's Office of Yavapai County and Heidi Hoover, the star reporter of *The Daily Pilot*, in a search for an unknown perpetrator.

Book 8: The Hunt for the Elusive Mastermind

(Coming Spring, 2021)

The mystery searchers embark on one of their strangest cases—the kidnapping of the wife of one of the city's most prominent bankers, and the baffling questions of who the bad guys actually were and what happened to the money.

Don't forget to check out

www.MysterySearchers.com

Register to receive *free* parent/reader study guides for each book in the series—valuable teaching and learning tools for middle-grade students and their parents.

You'll also find a wealth of information on the website: stills and video scenes of Prescott, reviews, press releases, rewards, and more. Plus I'll update you on new releases and other news.